Raves For the Work of ED McBAIN!

"McBain is so good he ought to be arrested."
—*Publishers Weekly*

"The best crime writer in the business."
—*Houston Post*

"The author delivers the goods: wired action scenes, dialogue that breathes, characters with hearts and characters that eat those hearts, and glints of unforgiving humor...Ed McBain owns this turf."
—*New York Times Book Review*

"You'll be engrossed by McBain's fast, lean prose."
—*Chicago Tribune*

"McBain has a great approach, great attitude, terrific style, strong plots, excellent dialogue, sense of place, and sense of reality."
—*Elmore Leonard*

"McBain is a top pro, at the top of his game."
—*Los Angeles Daily News*

"A virtuoso."
—*London Guardian*

"Vintage stuff. The dialogue is sharp, the plotting accomplished, and the prose bears the McBain stamp—uncluttered, unpretentious, ironic."
—*The Philadelphia Inquirer*

"If you're looking for a sure thing, pick this one up."
—*Syracuse Herald-American*

"A major contemporary writer...His prose [approaches] a kind of colloquial poetry."
—*William DeAndrea, Encyclopedia Mysteriosa*

"The McBain stamp: sharp dialogue and crisp plotting."
—*The Miami Herald*

"A master storyteller."
—*Washington Times*

"McBain keeps you reading and keeps you guessing... The book is a winner."
—*London Sunday Telegraph*

She drained her glass and went into the kitchen. When she came back, the bottle was in her hand. She looked at me, and her eyes held mine, and she said in a cold level voice, "Do you believe there are some things a person must do, right or wrong?"

I shrugged.

"I don't care what you believe," she said. "There's something I've got to do right now. I've got to get stinking blind drunk. Can you understand that?"

She'd picked the right person to ask. "I can understand it," I said, "but the police might not when they get here."

"The hell with the police," she said. "I'm going to get so drunk I can't stand. You can stay if you want to see it. If you'd rather not, then leave."

She poured three inches of straight bourbon over the ice in her glass. "Here's to murderers," she said, "the goddamn world is full of them." She knocked off the three inches and refilled the glass.

"Not too fast," I said, "or you'll get sick."

"I want it fast and hard," she said. "I want it to knock me down." She drank the refill and poured again, gagging a little as the stuff went down. Then she kicked off her high-heeled pumps. Then she put down the bottle and pulled off the half-slip, and then she went to sit by the window in bra and panties, her feet propped up on the window sill.

She killed the third drink and then tossed her long blonde hair over her shoulder and shot me a backward glance and flashed the most evil smile since Eve grinned at Adam with the apple in her teeth.

"Come here, Cordell," she said.

"What for?"

"Come here and kiss me..."

12|05
$7

The GUTTER
and
the GRAVE

by **Ed McBain**

A HARD CASE · CRIME NOVEL

HARD
CASE
CRIME

A HARD CASE CRIME BOOK
(HCC-015)
December 2005

Published by

Dorchester Publishing Co., Inc.
200 Madison Avenue
New York, NY 10016

in collaboration with Winterfall LLC

ISBN 0-8439-5587-2

The name "Hard Case Crime" and the Hard Case Crime logo
are trademarks of Winterfall LLC. Hard Case Crime books are
selected and edited by Charles Ardai.

Printed in the United States of America

Visit us on the web at www.HardCaseCrime.com

The new ones, the old ones, they're all now dedicated to the love of my life—my wife, Dragica.

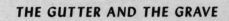

THE GUTTER AND THE GRAVE

Chapter One

The name is Cordell.

I'm a drunk. I think we'd better get that straight from the beginning. I drink because I want to drink. Sometimes I'm falling-down ossified, and sometimes I'm rosy-glow happy, and sometimes I'm cold sober—but not very often. I'm usually drunk, and I live where being drunk isn't a sin, though it's sometimes a crime when the police go on a purity drive. I live on New York's Bowery.

There's some talk that now with the Third Avenue El demolished, real estate values will soar and the city will clean out the Bowery and make it a respectable high-priced business district. All right. When they do, I'll move elsewhere. There's always an elsewhere for people who are running from something. I'm running from a ghost. The ghost is named Matt Cordell.

There's a little park just outside Cooper Union. During the school term, the park is full of art and engineering students. The young girls come out in their paint-daubed smocks and puff on their cigarettes as if this is the last smoke before the firing squad takes over. It's fun to watch the kids because they're burning more than cigarettes—they're burning life, they're burning it in big blazing holocausts and loving every minute of it. It's great to be alive, I guess. I never go to that little park during the school term. I go there in the summer, though. The park is empty then. You can sit on one of the benches and look at the statue of Peter Cooper and feel protected and cloistered in the middle of a giant throbbing city. Once in a while, a cop will come along and tell you to move on. But most of the time, you can sit there and be alone in the center of a crowd.

I was there when Johnny Bridges found me. I wasn't drunk. I was feeling like tying on a stiff one because New York City in the summertime is possibly the hottest place in the world. I can't understand why tourists come here. It's a wonderful place to live, but who'd want to visit it? I was sitting in the park thinking of cool civilized drinks like Tom Collinses and Planter's Punches and then thinking about what *I'd* drink—an uncool, uncivilized pint of cheap booze. That was when Johnny Bridges walked up.

"Matt?" he said.

I didn't recognize him at first. He'd put on some weight around the middle, and his features were a little thicker. It took me a few moments to place the broad shoulders and the brown eyes, the narrow thin lips and the sharply sweeping nose. Then the name came back from somewhere in my memory, Johnny Bridges, and I looked at him with new interest. He was about my age, I guessed, thirty-two or thirty-three. I hadn't seen him in ten years.

"Matt Cordell?" he said.

"Yeah."

"How've you been?" he said, smiling. "You remember me, don't you? I'm…"

"Yeah," I said. "What's on your mind?"

"Okay if I sit down?" he asked.

"It's a free country."

He sat on the bench alongside me. He tried not to notice the shabby wrinkled suit I was wearing, or the soiled shirt, or the fact that I hadn't shaved in a week. He tried not to notice my red-rimmed eyes, too, but he didn't succeed in hiding his initial shock or the slow adjustment he was making to my appearance. I don't know what he expected, but this wasn't the Matt Cordell he'd known ten years ago. Nervously, he fished into his jacket pocket and extended a package of cigarettes to me.

"Smoke?" he said.

I took a cigarette and he lighted it for me, returning the package to his pocket after he'd taken one for himself. He was wearing a blue seersucker suit with a red tie. I figured he was working for a Madison Avenue advertising agency or a bank. He looked very neat and very clean-shaven and very Esquire magazine-ish. It probably made him itchy just sitting there beside me.

"How have you been, Matt?" he asked.

"Just dandy," I said. "And you?"

"Fine. Oh, fine," Johnny said.

"That's good."

"Yeah, that's…" He let the sentence trail. We sat in

silence for a little while. I don't believe in pushing a man. He'd come looking for me, and I'd have been delighted if he hadn't found me. If he had anything on his mind, he'd get to it in his own time. If he had nothing to say, he could leave as soon as he finished his cigarette.

"I read about you," Johnny said. "In the newspapers."

"Yeah?"

"That was a terrible thing," he said. "I mean, the whole business. The thing with your wife, and then the police taking away your…"

"Let's forget it, Johnny," I said.

"From what I heard…I mean, I heard you were a good detective."

"I was," I said.

"When they take away a man's license…"

"He stops being a private detective," I said. "He moves to the Bowery. Okay? Can we drop it now?"

"It must have been quite a blow," Johnny said.

"It's always a blow to find out your wife's unfaithful," I said, and then I stood up. "I'll see you, Johnny." I started to walk away, and he put his hand on my arm.

"No, look, wait a minute," he said. "I'm sorry. I didn't realize it still bothered you."

"It does," I said. It still bothered me. It bothered the hell out of me, and I didn't feel like sitting there discussing it with a guy I hadn't seen in ten years.

"Okay," he said, "we'll forget it, okay?"

I almost laughed out loud. Forget it! I'd spent the

past five years trying to do just that. And now Johnny Bridges spoke the magic words, and we'd forget it. Bang! Johnny Bridges, Sorcerer's Apprentice.

"What do you want, Johnny?" I said. "I was on my way to getting drunk."

"I need your help, Matt," he said.

"*My* help? How can I help you?"

"You used to be a detective…"

"Used to is right. I'm not any longer. I have no license. You said you read the newspapers. All right, you know they yanked my license."

"Yes, I know. But still, you used to practice…and you were good."

"So?"

"So…I…need help, Matt."

"Are you talking about an investigation?" I said.

"Yes. Sort of."

"Count me out," I said. I started to go again. He came up off the bench and stepped into my path.

"Matt, listen…I'd go to a regular detective agency, but I can't afford it."

"That's unfortunate," I said. "Why don't you go to the police?"

"Because I don't want this thing to…look, can I explain it to you a minute? Can I just explain it to you?"

"I'm getting thirsty," I told him.

"I'll buy you a drink. Will you listen then?"

"Sure. Come on."

We went to a bar on Fourteenth Street. I didn't take him to any of the Bowery places, which were a lot less

expensive, because I thought they might embarrass
him. The bar we went to served both bankers and
bums. We went to a booth at the back. Johnny ordered
a gin and tonic. I ordered rye neat. When the drinks
came, I threw mine down and asked for another. I
threw that one down, too, and Johnny ordered a third
for me and then began sipping at his gin-tonic.

"So what's the story?" I said.

"I'm a tailor," he told me.

This shouldn't have surprised me because his father
had been a tailor, but I guess the seersucker suit threw
me. Besides, in this day and age, you don't think of
young men entering professions like tailoring or
baking or cobbling. You just don't.

"I'm in business with another guy," he said. "Up in
the old neighborhood. Maybe you remember him.
Dom Archese?"

"No, I don't remember him."

"Well, that's because he's older than us. He used to
hang around with Frankie Di Luca, that bunch. He's a
wonderful guy, Dom. Married, settled down. You
know. But…" He stopped and shook his head. The bar
was silent except for the whir of a giant fan in one
corner of the room. The fan didn't help the heat much.
Even in his seersucker suit, Johnny Bridges was beginning to sweat.

"You're having trouble with Dom?" I said. "Is
that it?"

"Well, I don't know, that's the problem. I mean, he's
a wonderful guy, Matt, honest he is. He didn't know

anything about running a tailor shop when we first started. I knew it from my father…well, you remember him."

"Yes."

"Sure. But Dom didn't know a thing. He'd just got married, and he was looking for a good steady business, so he asked if I could use a partner in the shop. The business came to me when my father—God rest his soul—passed away, you see."

"I see. So you took Dom in, is that right?"

"Yeah. Well, I didn't *take* him in exactly. He bought in. After all, it was an established business with a lot of steady customers. Actually, I was glad to have a partner. The work was really too much. Even now, we have to hire a presser. And Dom caught on right away. I mean, he still doesn't do any of the actual tailoring work, that's not something you pick up overnight, you know. But he's great with the customers, and he knows how to press, and eventually he'll learn how to sew, too. Not that there's very much of that to be done, tell the truth. Nowadays, a tailor shop is mostly dry-cleaning and pressing. Except for sewing up a ripped seam every now and then. You know how it is."

"So this Dom Archese—is it Dominic?"

"Yes, Dominic. Everybody calls him Dom, though."

"This Dom Archese is a married man who bought into the tailor shop because he wanted something sturdy and solid and apparently had a little money to play around with."

"Five thousand dollars," Johnny said. "That's what it cost him. I probably could have got more, but actually I needed a partner and was glad to have him. He's a wonderful guy."

"You said that before."

"Well, he is."

"Then what's the trouble?"

"Well, I don't know. Dom's not a rich man, you understand. That five grand was probably his life savings. He's got some government bonds, and maybe a little in the bank, and some insurance to take care of Christine—God forbid anything should happen to him."

"Christine? Is that his wife?"

"Yes. But what I'm trying to say is that he isn't a rich man, and maybe he's in some kind of financial trouble or something, I don't know. It's the only way I can figure it."

"Figure what?"

"The thefts," Johnny said.

"Someone's been stealing something?"

"Yes," Johnny said. "From the cash register."

"How much? Large amounts?"

"No. No, that's just it. The thefts have been small. Ten dollars at a time. Sometimes fifteen dollars. Until this last one."

"How much was the last one?"

"Fifty dollars."

"That still isn't very large," I said.

"Well, it's large enough to be serious," Johnny said.

"How much has been stolen altogether?"

"Two hundred and thirty-five dollars."

"Over how long a period of time?"

"About six months, I think. In any case, that was when I noticed the first shortage."

"Did you tell Dom about it?"

"Yes. He said I probably added wrong. Then, when I found the second theft, a couple of weeks later, I told him again."

"And what did he say that time?"

"The same thing. He's either a very trusting person, Dom, or else…" Johnny shrugged. "I don't know what to think."

"Who else works in the shop?"

"A kid named Dave Ryan. He's our presser."

"Does he handle the cash register at all?"

"No."

"But he could get into it when you or Dom aren't around, couldn't he?"

"No. If both of us are out of the shop, we lock the register."

"Then he does sometimes work alone in the shop? When both of you are gone?"

"Yes. He presses at night sometimes. I told you, there's a lot of work to be done."

"But the register is locked?"

"Yes."

"So you figure it's Dom who's been dipping into the till?"

"That's right."

"Well, what do you want from me?" I said.

"Matt, I don't know what to do. How can I blow the whistle on my partner and friend? How can I go to the police? If he's taking the money, he must have a damn good reason."

"Why don't you talk to him? Tell him…"

"And suppose I'm wrong? Suppose it isn't him? Suppose…I don't know…suppose somebody's sneaking in at night or something? Jesus, I don't know what to do, Matt. That's why I came down to see you. I've been all over the Bowery looking for you. Finally, some guy told me I might find you in that park outside the school. Won't you help me, Matt?"

"By doing what?"

"Come up to the shop. Look over the register, look over the windows. Maybe somebody's getting in at night and forcing the drawer. I can't tell, but I'm sure you could."

"Do you ever leave any money in the register at night?"

"Yes. Usually about fifty bucks or so. Just enough to start the next day. It saves the trouble of taking it out and then bringing it back in the morning."

"Mmmm. Then there is the possibility…"

"Will you help me, Matt?"

I thought about it for a while. Did I want to go back to the old neighborhood, see people I'd known when I was a kid? Did I want more memories to add to the memory I already carried, the memory of first meeting Toni, that goddamn corny meeting as she was coming off the Triborough Bridge, laughing, her blonde hair caught by the November wind, walking with the Randall's Island football crowd, carrying a pennant in her hand? Did I want that memory to come welling back, and with it all the other ghosts, all the shadows I'd been drinking away for five years?

"No," I said to Johnny. "I'm busy. I can't help you."

"Busy doing what?" Johnny asked. He paused, seemed to weigh his next question, and then said, "Getting drunk?"

"Yes," I said, "getting drunk. Do you have any objections?"

"It seems to me…"

"It seems to me a smart man stops when he's ahead," I told him. "I'd hate like hell to have to knock down an old neighbor."

"You talk a good game, Matt," he said, and he stood up. He reached into his pocket for some change to leave on the table. "What are you afraid of?" he said. "The police? This wouldn't be an official investigation. It would just be an old friend doing a favor."

"When did we become such good old buddies?" I said.

"For Christ's sake, we grew up together."

"Does that make us brothers? Go to the police. Or else get yourself a bona fide private detective. Don't come running to a Bowery bum."

"Is that what you are, Matt?"

"What the hell did you think I was? A society swordsman? A pedigreed dog trainer? I'm a bum. Me. Matthew Cordell, bum. I sleep in flophouses or on park benches when I can't afford a pad. I'm drunk twenty-five hours out of twenty-four, and I get my whiskey money by panhandling. I'm a bum. Do you want me to yell hallelujah?"

He shook his head and looked at me. "I didn't think it was possible," he said. "I didn't think a dame…"

"Shut up, Johnny."

"…could take a guy who was a *man* and turn him into…"

"Shut up!"

"Sure. Thanks for listening, Matt. I'll work it out some way. Thanks a lot."

"Get the pity out of your eyes," I said. "I don't need it."

"You need something, pal," he said.

"Oh, go the hell back to 118th Street. Who asked you to come down here, anyway? Who needs you?"

"I need you," he said.

"Sure."

"I do. Matt…please. Won't you help me?" He put his arm on my sleeve, and I've never been able to kick a man in the teeth when he suddenly begins begging. "Please, Matt, I'm…I'm ready to lose my mind with this damn thing. Please. Help me."

"No."

"I'll pay you. I can't afford much but…"

"I don't want your money."

"Then will you help me? Will you please…"

"Jesus Christ, can't you leave me alone?" I said.

The table was suddenly silent. Johnny kept looking at me. I kept looking at my hands.

In a small voice, I said, "Can't you just leave me alone?" He didn't answer. He kept staring at me. Finally, I raised my head and met his eyes. "I'll…I'll just take a look at the…the windows and doors," I said. "And the cash register. Just to let you know if…if someone's been getting in at night. But that's all. I don't want…"

"Thank you, Matt," he said.

The sky had turned black outside. Clouds had moved in over the river and were banked overhead now, ready to burst. There was a smell in the air, the sweet air-rushing smell a city gets just before an electric storm. The lights in some of the shops had already come on as the city grew darker. It was going to rain like hell.

We caught a cab and headed uptown. The tailor shop was on First Avenue between 118th and 119th. It was just a small shop, with the usual dry-cleaning posters in the window, the posters that somehow never look professional but seem to have been run off by an art student in a basement. There was also a small sign in the window which read: WE DO EXPERT HAND TAILORING. A heavy padlock hung on the front door.

"Nobody here?" I said.

Johnny looked at his watch. "We close at six," he said. "Dom is probably home already."

"Were you in the shop today?"

"Yes." Johnny took out a key ring and began searching for the right key.

"When?" I said.

He found the key and unlocked the padlock. "I came in around noon, and left at two. I went down to the Bowery. To look for you." He swung open the door and snapped on the lights. The rain had still not started, but it wouldn't be long now. "This is it," he said.

The shop was the kind of shop you don't find around much anymore. Two sewing machines were near the window, and opposite them was the counter over which business was done, the cash register at the extreme right. Behind that was a row of cabinets in which the finished clothes hung, waiting to be claimed. A curtained doorway bisected the clothing racks. I assumed the doorway led to the back of the shop. I also assumed the pressing was done in the back.

"There's the cash register," Johnny said.

I went over to it and studied it for a few minutes. "It doesn't look to me as if it's ever been forced," I said. "Where's your key?"

He took out his key ring again and handed me the key. I unlocked the register and opened it. As Johnny had said, there was about fifty dollars in small bills and change left in the register to start the new day. There were no marks on the drawer. I slammed it shut, locked it again, and handed the key ring back to Johnny.

"Is that the only entrance door?" I said, gesturing at the front door.

"No, there's another at the back of the shop. And a lot of windows that open on the airshaft."

"Let's take a look," I said.

We were moving toward the curtained doorway when the rain started. It started with a crackling streak of lightning and an answering bellow of thunder, and then the rain poured down suddenly in giant spattering drops, sweeping across the streets and pavement. Outside, people began running for shelter. Another lightning streak shattered the sky.

"It's going to be a bad storm," Johnny said.

"Yeah."

"Come on, I'll take you in back."

He swept aside the curtains. I followed him into the back of the shop. It was dark back there, and I almost stumbled on a basket of unpressed clothes. Then Johnny snapped on the light.

The first thing I saw was the giant pressing machine with its levers and cloth-covered pads, gaping open like the jaws of a monster. The next thing I saw was the man sprawled against the wall opposite the machine. The man was in his early forties, wearing a white dress shirt with the collar unbuttoned and the sleeves rolled up. The front of his shirt was red with blood that flowed from two holes in his chest. A piece of tailor's chalk was in the man's right hand.

Scrawled in chalk on the wall behind him was an arrow and the arrow pointed to the initials J.B. which had also been chalked onto the wall in a shaky hand.

I guess Johnny Bridges saw the initials at the same time I did because he let out a short sharp scream and then whirled to me, his eyes wide with terror.

Chapter Two

"Goodbye, Johnny," I said, and I turned and started for the curtained doorway. He clutched my arm with the strength that sometimes comes with total panic, swinging me around and then grabbing both my arms and staring at me and not speaking for a few seconds, just staring at my face with his eyes wide and a small tic at the corner of his mouth.

And then he said, "Matt...I...I...I...," the words coming out like short bursts from a sighing machine gun.

"Johnny," I said, "I don't know what this is all about. I'm willing to believe you didn't know that guy was lying dead by the wall when you came to fetch me. I'm willing to believe the only thing on your mind was the cash being swiped from..."

"That's the truth! I didn't know..."

"But the guy *is* dead, and I'm here, and man, when the cops start seeping out of the woodwork, I don't *want* to be here. I want to be as far away from here as I can get. So long, pal, it was nice." I started to go again, and his fingers tightened on my arms. "Let go of me, Johnny."

"Matt, you can't leave now. That's Dom! That man is Dom, my partner."

"I don't care if he's the Pope. He's dead. Look, Johnny, I've had cops—up to here, I've had them. I don't want them anymore."

A look of desperation came into Johnny's eyes, and then the look fled before an idea, and the idea claimed the eyes so that they became narrow and crafty.

"You can't leave," he said. "I'll tell the police you were with me when I found the body. They'll come after you."

I didn't say anything. I just watched him, and then I nodded, but I still didn't say anything. Outside, the rain swept the streets relentlessly. At the front of the shop, over the steady wash of the storm, I could hear the ticking of a big clock.

Finally I said, "Is that why you came to find me?"

"What do you mean?"

"So you'd have someone with you when you accidentally 'discovered' the body?"

"You don't believe that, Matt."

I didn't, actually. If he'd wanted someone he could put on an act for, he wouldn't go digging up a Bowery bum. Besides, those initials on the wall were J.B., and I didn't think any murderer was nuts enough to deliberately point the finger at himself and then try to register shock and surprise before a witness. I'd known of killers who'd made a point of directing suspicion toward themselves, but only after they'd set up an airtight alibi that would immediately dispel any suspicion when investigated. But those chalked initials on the wall were almost a dying man's declaration, and the declaration of a man about to die—where it concerns his attacker—is admissible as court evidence and very often leads to a conviction. Johnny Bridges, whether he knew it or not, had read the writing on the wall. I'd read it, too, and I didn't want any damn part of it. But if he planned to tell the police I'd been with him when he discovered the body, it would look worse for me if I ran.

Did you ever have the feeling that you wanted to go, and yet…?

"Did you kill him?" I said.

"No."

"Your initials are on the wall. A big arrow points to them. The police will assume Archese put them there before he died."

"I know."

"Do you know anyone else with those initials?"

"No…not offhand. Matt, what am I going to….?"

"Did you get along with Archese?"

"Yes. Matt, for Christ's sake."

"You said you were in the shop between twelve and two. Is that right, Johnny?"

"Yes."

"Was Archese here?"

"Yes."

"Was anyone else here?"

"No."

"What did you do then?"

"I stopped in to say hello to Christine. That's Dom's wife. As a matter of fact, he asked me to stop by. He'd left a check for her, and he wasn't sure she knew where it was. So I went by to tell her."

"Why didn't he phone her?"

"I don't know."

"Does he have a phone at home?"

"Yes. I guess he could have called her. But he was busy pressing, so maybe he thought it'd be easier if I stopped by. I had to pass that way, anyway."

"How long did you stay with her?"

"About a half-hour."

"Then what?"

"Then I started for the Bowery. To look for you."

"And Archese was alive at two o'clock when you left him, right?"

"Yes."

"Do you often come into the shop for just two hours?"

"Tuesday is my day off. I only came in to see how things were going."

"Did you and Archese argue?"

"No, we just chatted for a while."

"Did you *ever* argue?"

"No. We got along fine."

"What did you chat about this afternoon?"

"The cash register thefts."

"Did you accuse him?"

"No. We just talked about it, and that was when I decided to come down to see you."

"Do you own a gun?"

"Yes."

"Where is it?"

"In the drawer out front."

"You'd better let me see it."

We went out to the front of the shop. It was still raining, but the thunder and lightning had stopped. The rain pressed against the big plate-glass window, melting it. Johnny went to a drawer near the cash register, and pulled it open and moved some papers and a scissors aside. He reached clear to the back of the drawer and then turned to me.

"It's gone," he said.

"What kind of a gun was it?"

"A Smith and Wesson .38."

"Do you have a permit for it?"

"Yes."

"Carry or premises?"

"Premises. The gun never left that drawer. The store was held up once, right after my father passed away. So I got a permit and bought a gun."

"Don't be surprised if the slugs they dig out of Archese were fired from a .38 Smith and Wesson," I said.

"What are we going to do, Matt?" he said.

The panic had left his eyes. He was watching me with calm intelligence now. For all practical purposes, there was no longer a dead man in the back room. We were simply two level-headed gentlemen discussing a course of action on something of slightly more than everyday importance. I watched him and then told him what I thought.

"I don't want to get involved with the police again. I had enough of the police that time with my wife. I'm sure they remember me, and maybe yanking my license wasn't enough for them. I'm willing to make a deal with you, Johnny."

"What's the deal?"

"Leave me out of this. You came back to the store alone and found the body alone. I wasn't with you."

"What good will lying do me?"

"A lot of good. When the police see those initials, they're going to think they've got an open-and-shut. They're going to lock you up faster than they can say 'Suspicion of homicide.' That puts you on the inside and the real murderer on the outside. The cops will then begin their investigation. The D.A.'s office will do its best to uncover facts that will clinch the prosecution. They've already got what amounts to a dying man's declaration. They may also have two bullets that came from your gun. With a murderer already in the pokey, they're not going to try too hard to find another one."

"I still don't understand," Johnny said.

"Then I'll spell it for you. You'll tell your lawyer you're innocent, but he certainly isn't going to start a private investigation. He's going to build his defense on lack of motive or opportunity. If those bullets were fired from your gun, the prosecution can easily show 'means.' Lack of motive is a weak defense. As for opportunity, you could have come into this shop anytime during the day and put the blocks to your partner."

"How? I was with Christine and then with you."

"Why did you come to see me?"

"Because…"

"Because you suspected your partner of being a crook."

"Yes."

"Couldn't you have argued about this? Couldn't this have been your motive for killing him?"

"Oh, Matt, for Christ's sake…"

"People have been killed for less."

"But…"

"If you leave me out of it, your opportunity angle is weakened, true. You won't have the alibi of having spent the afternoon with me. But remember, Johnny, there's only your word for the time you spent *before* you found me in that park outside Cooper. That was about five o'clock, wasn't it?"

"Yes."

"All right, where the hell were you between two-thirty, when you left Christine, and five, when you found me?"

"I was looking for you! I told you that! I must have asked a hundred people on the Bowery where I could find you."

"Think they'd make good witnesses for the defense?"

"Oh Jesus, I don't know. I just don't know."

"Actually, I spent a little more than an hour with you. We got here a little after six, didn't we?" Johnny nodded. "So if Archese was killed anytime between two, when you left the shop, and five, when you found me, you're still in the soup. And obviously he *was* killed between those times. If you drag me in, I'm a weak alibi. And also a guy the cops don't particularly like."

"So what's your deal?"

"Leave me out of it," I said. "Leave me out of it, and you've hired yourself a private detective."

"To do what?"

"To find the person who really killed your partner."

"I don't know."

"Or else play it your way," I said. "Drag me into it, and take your chances with a case the D.A. can really go to town with."

Johnny thought for a few minutes. Then he said, "Okay. It's a deal. What do I do?"

"The first thing you do is call the police. Tell them you just got to the shop and you found your partner dead in the back room."

"Do I call Homicide?"

"No. Just ask the operator for the police. Your call'll go to Headquarters and then be relayed to the local precinct. Detectives from the squad there will handle the case. Homicide'll be informed, but they don't come out on the case."

"And I don't tell them anything about you?"

"No. Tell them you went downtown shopping. You looked around all afternoon, but didn't find anything you liked. It's weak, but no weaker than searching the Bowery for an old friend. And this way you won't have to mention the thefts. This way you won't give them a motive."

"All right."

"In the meantime, I'll start asking around. You'd better give me his wife's address. You said he had insurance, didn't you?"

"Yes."

"Did his wife know there was a gun in that drawer?"

"Yes, I think so."

"Then I'd better talk to her. Where does she live?" Johnny gave me the address and I wrote it down. "About this presser," I said. "Work for you long?"

"About six months."

"What's his name?"

"Dave Ryan."

"And his address?" Johnny gave it to me. "Did he get along with Dom?"

"Yes. He's just a kid. A nice guy."

"Okay. Are we clear on our deal?" Johnny nodded. "Then go call the police. I'll see you in jail."

And I left the shop.

I could remember my last big bout with the police very clearly. Walking in the slow steady rain that had replaced the earlier fury of the storm, I could remember all of it as if it had happened yesterday and not five years ago. It was an easy thing to remember. The memory didn't just come back, it was always there, always present, always ready to be released by a suddenly recognized song, or the scent of a familiar perfume, or even a cloud formation sometimes, or sometimes just the city, just the physical being of the city and the knowledge that Toni and I had once lived together here, loved together here.

I'm a slum boy, you see, I was born and raised on the upper East Side of Manhattan before the Puerto Ricans began to infiltrate that part of the city. I was raised among other people who could not speak English too well, and I was a part of their slow adjustment to the new world. That section of town was all Irish and Italian at the time. My father was a big mick with a big brogue who'd come to America to earn a living. He married an Irish lass who still believed the stories she'd heard in the old country about good fairies and hobgoblins and dryads. It wasn't easy being Irish. It's never easy being anything that isn't what everybody else is.

But it wasn't such a bad place to grow up in. The worst neighborhoods never seem so bad or dangerous to the people who live in them. I wanted to go to college, but I never got there because my father died and I had to support the house. I thought of becoming a cop, but I never became that either because I was making more money working for a haberdasher than I could have made as a rookie. When my mother died, I became a private detective. Just like that. I mean it. Just like that. I applied for a job, and I got one. I'm a pretty big fellow, six-one and broad in the shoulders. The work I did with the agency for the first few years consisted mostly of breaking down bedroom doors and

snapping pictures of adult delinquents in various compromising postures. I didn't like the work. I quit and
formed my own agency, and it was becoming a recognized one when I met Toni.

Toni McAllister.

It's a good name. It still excites me. It excited me
the first time I heard it, as if I were waiting to hear that
name all my life, and suddenly there it was. And the
girl went with it. She came off the Triborough waving
a football pennant, that long blonde hair caught on the
November breeze, caught and held there, a spun gold
web. Green eyes that echoed the green scarf around
her throat. A leopardskin coat, and she wore it as if the
animal were still alive, a sleek study in motion, trim
and clean, full thighs beneath the woolen dress,
slender ankles and the clatter of high-heeled shoes,
the subtle swing of leg and thigh and hip, Toni
McAllister with a bright orange pennant and a bunch
of college boys smoking pipes and wearing tweeds.
The smell of perfume and class, both delicate scents,
both wafted on the air insinuatingly, touching me,
reaching for me, Matt Cordell, the kid from the wrong
part of the East Side, but not a kid anymore, a man
who watched this invasion from the outer space of
upper Park Avenue, Toni McAllister, a fresh breeze in
the garbage-smell of the slums.

She stopped before me where I was leaning against
the concrete support of the ramp. Her lips pulled back
over small even white teeth, widening into a smile.
There was another scent now, the smell of alcohol, and

then her voice came and there was a taunting lilt to it, a tease that was repeated in the flashing green eyes.

"Are you a Princeton or a Rutgers?" she said. She continued smiling. She leaned close to me, and our eyes locked, green with brown.

"Come on, Toni," one of the college boys said.

"Go to hell," she told him without looking over her shoulder. "Are you a Princeton or a Rutgers?" she said again.

"I'm a Peter Stuyvesant High School," I said.

She laughed. She threw back her head and laughed, and one of the college boys said, "Come on, Toni, will you?"

"Princeton won," she said to me. "I'm a Princeton. If you're a Princeton, I'll buy you a drink."

"I'm not a Princeton," I told her.

"That's a damn shame," she said. "Don't say I didn't ask."

"I thought the *gentleman* asked," I said.

"Are you a gentleman?"

"Not usually. But I'm asking. Let *me* buy *you* a drink."

"How original," Toni said, and she hooked her arm through mine, and we left three college boys standing on the pavement waving pennants.

That was the beginning.

The beginning and the end are clearest in my mind. What came in between was something I'd never known before, and it's impossible to pick any isolated experience and say This was more meaningful than that, or This caused more pleasure than that. It was all a high-speeding jet plane, and the wash dissolved behind it; it was Matt Cordell and Toni McAllister and the hell with the world. It was Park Avenue mixed with the slums, it was cocktail parties and pool parlors, theatre openings and all-night movies on Forty-Second Street. It was her world and mine, mixed like a Zombie, four thousand kinds of rum, but blended because underneath the exotic name, it was all rum. It was talking about everything under the sun, and it was long periods of silence, the ferry ride to Staten Island with the lights of Manhattan looming against the sky and Toni against me with my arms around her, a cutting wind blowing in over the bay. It was Matt Cordell and Toni McAllister, the impossible suddenly possible.

And after a year, it became Toni Cordell.

And then, of course, the end.

I'd hired a man named Dave Parker to supplement the three men already working for me. He was a clever guy who wasn't afraid of tackling any case. We got along fine. It was one of those working arrangements where we both seemed to think together. Toni liked him, too. Then I went out of town on a case for about two weeks. I came home one night without calling Toni first—the old bit, so corny it makes me vomit, but it happened, as real as life: hubby coming home unexpectedly, the light burning in the bedroom upstairs, the big surprise grin on hubby's face, and then the grin turning to ashes because Toni is in the arms of another man, Toni is in the arms of Dave Parker.

I hit him with a .45.

I had a license for the gun, of course, and I pulled it from the shoulder holster, and I went at him, and I kept hitting him because the son-of-a-bitch hadn't only taken my wife of four months, he had taken a dream, and dreams are the one thing you should never steal from a man. And so I tried to reconstruct a demolished dream by destroying the demolisher, and all I did was destroy myself.

The police were so kind, the bastards. They understood completely, but they took away my license and my gun and my pride.

End of story. Add a Mexican divorce. Toni Cordell becomes Toni McAllister again. A little too old for the Princeton-Rutgers routine, a little less sleek, the younger competition springing up in the plush Manhattan bistros, but still with the challenge in her green eyes, still with the dazzling even smile and the narrow ankles and the educated hip-and-leg stalk of a leopard.

End of story.

Add a guy with a shattered dream and no profession and a trunkful of memories, painful, the climactic memory the worst of all, a guy who wished *he'd* have been beaten with a .45, truly destroyed, beaten to a pulp until there was nothing left but the memory of a man. Matt Cordell, memory. I drifted to the Bowery. There were a lot of people trying to forget there. And maybe Dave Parker's face healed, but Matt Cordell carried scars that would never heal. Alcohol is good for scars; it's an antiseptic.

Now, five years later, I walked where I'd first met her. I was about to do a job again. I felt no pride, I felt no anticipation, I felt no excitement. All that went out of me the night I walked into that bedroom and found my wife Toni with another man's hands twisted in her long blonde hair.

Chapter Three

Christine Archese was a blonde.

She opened the door a crack, looked out at me, and left the chain on. I'm not a wholesome sight to behold. Somewhere under the growth of my beard there is what Toni once called "an Irish boulder jaw," but it is barely recognizable. My eyes are brown, but they bear the telltale red of the whiskey drinker. I pass for a man sometimes, but only because I once belonged to the human race.

"What do you want?" she said. There was no fright in her voice. I saw level blue eyes in the crack of the door, those and the blonde hair.

"Johnny Bridges sent me," I said. "I'm a friend of his."

"What's your name?"

"Matt Cordell."

"I don't know you."

"Open the door, Christine," I said. "I'm harmless. And Johnny's in trouble."

She hesitated a moment, and then took off the chain. Her eyes swept me quickly as I walked into the apartment. The apartment was furnished with nice Third Avenue department store furniture. It was spot-

lessly clean. Christine Archese led me into the living
room of the railroad flat and then offered me a chair. I
sat. She was a tall girl with a magnificent bosom and
good hips, a little thick in the waist and legs, a strong
girl with strong hands and jaw, a mouth full and meaningful, eyes like the blue steel of an automatic.

"What kind of trouble is Johnny in?" she asked.

"Let me ask you something first."

"What do you want to ask me?"

"Was Johnny here today?"

"Yes."

"When?"

"Two, two-thirty. I don't remember exactly. Why?"

"Did he say where he was going when he left?"

"Yes. To look up a friend who'd been a private…"
She stopped and sudden recognition crossed her face.
"Did you say your name was Matt Cordell?"

"Yes."

"Oh. Oh sure. Well, he…" She studied my face
more closely. "Of course. I should have remembered.
Your picture was all over the papers when it happened." She nodded. "Still not over it, huh?"

"Let's drop it," I said.

"Sure. Did Johnny find you?"

"He found me."

"Well, any friend of Johnny's is a friend of mine,"
she said dubiously. "Would you like a cup of coffee?"

"Maybe you'd better listen to why I'm here first."

"Why are you here?"

"Your husband is dead. Someone shot him."

The reaction is always the same. I would rather swim underwater and attach nuclear weapons to Russian battleships than tell a person a loved one is dead. There is nothing funny about death. It always hits a person right between the eyes, an awesome shock that knocks the breath from the chest and suddenly fills the eyes with agony. Nor is the reaction any different when a person is faking. It is almost impossible to tell fake shock from real shock, and so the reaction to news of death is always the same.

Christine Archese reeled back from the blow of my words. I might just as well have struck her. Her mouth opened, and her head jerked back, and then her eyes were knifed with pain, and she brought her hands together in a sudden unconscious gesture and she said, "No!"

"I'm sorry," I said.

She began crying then, suddenly and fitfully. The big breasts heaved, and the strong woman was not that anymore. She was a little girl faced with irremediable sorrow. The tears streaked down her cheeks, and she looked for a handkerchief and found none, and then she ran from the room and into the kitchen and unashamedly bawled into a dish towel. I sat in the living room. The rain outside had stopped. The apartment was silent except for the agonizing sound of Christine Archese weeping in the kitchen. I wished I had a drink.

She came back into the living room in a little while. Her mascara was streaked and her face was red and swollen. But she was a woman with good facial bones, and crying did not rob her of the near-beauty that was hers. She sat opposite me very primly and very stiffly. It seemed as if she were trying now to cover what she considered an unforgivable breach in a behavior pattern she had long ago established for herself. This was not a delicately feminine woman. This was not a petite, pouting, fragile china doll who blushed prettily and insisted on candle-lit sex on clean sheets. This was a big woman, peasant stock, a woman who filled every corner of a bed, a woman who had not wept in a long time. And so now, coming back into the living room, she sat with her back stiff and the big bosom thrust forward high and proud, her knees and feet close together, her chin lifted, the fine bones of her face glistening wetly.

"I'm sorry," she said. She was not apologizing to me. She was apologizing to herself.

"It's not a sin to cry," I said.

"Isn't it?"

"Not when you've lost someone you loved."

"How do you know?" she said.

"I've lost," I told her.

"And have you cried?"

"I've cried." Our eyes locked. "Yes, I've cried."

"Who killed him?" she asked.

"I don't know."

"Johnny?"

"Why do you say that?"

"Because you said he was in trouble. Did he kill Dom?"

"I don't know." I told her about the initials on the wall, and she listened attentively, nodding all the while, her hands clasped on her firm lap, her shoulders back.

"I don't think Johnny did it," she said when I had finished. "Why should he?"

"Did he tell you why he wanted to find me?"

"The cash register thefts, do you mean?"

"Yes."

"He told me. He certainly didn't suspect Dom."

"Did Dom ever discuss the thefts with you?"

"No."

"Isn't that a little odd?"

"Well, you see…"

I didn't see, and I was waiting to see, but a knock sounded on the door just then. Christine rose to open it. I didn't see who was standing in the doorframe. I knew only that it was a woman, and then Christine threw herself into the girl's arms and began wailing again. Together, they went into the kitchen, and I heard her yelling, "Dom is dead, oh my God, what am I going to do," and the other woman tried to hush her and console her, and I was left, sitting alone in the living room again playing "Here's the church, and here's the steeple" with my hands. They were out in the kitchen for five minutes, Christine crying, and the other girl trying to sympathize. Then they came back into the living room. I didn't have to be told who the other girl was. She was Christine's sister. I'd have bet a pint of wine on it.

She had the same blonde hair. She wore it long, flowing to her shoulders. She had the same excellently boned face, the same startlingly high cheekbones, the straight regal nose, the hard blue eyes. Her mouth was almost too perfectly formed, a gracefully curving upper lip and a full pouting lower lip. She was slightly smaller than her sister, but she still added up to a very big girl. Her throat swept sharply to her rising breasts, caught in a cheap white sweater; a narrow waist pulled in abruptly, bound constrictingly with a black leather belt; the hips flaring out below that, childbirth hips covered with a black skirt taut over firm thighs and good legs. She was no older than twenty-two, and I figured she had at least ten years on her sister. She studied me with unmasked distaste. This was a girl who was used to men, and she didn't like them bearded and rumpled. She made me feel as if I should run to take a bath. I didn't.

"This is my sister, Laraine," Christine said.

I stood up. "How do you do," I said. "I'm Matt…"

"Sit down before you fall down," Laraine said.

"Laraine!" her sister said sharply.

"Are you turning your living room into a flophouse?" Laraine said.

"This man is here to…"

"I don't care why he's here," Laraine said. "I know his kind. He should be ashamed of himself."

"Please forgive my sister."

"I can take care of myself, thanks," I said. "I'm sorry I offended you, young lady," I told Laraine.

"Matt Cordell, the big private eye!" Laraine said. "Look at him! A bum! Nothing but a flophouse bum."

"That's right," I said.

"What do you want? Why'd you come back to the East side?"

"To find a killer, it seems."

"Do you expect to find him here?"

"Maybe. Where were *you* all day?"

"What!"

"You heard me."

"Are you trying to say…?"

"I'm not trying to say anything. Somebody killed Dom Archese. I don't know who. A woman can pull a trigger as well as a man. That's the wonderful thing about guns. They're great equalizers in more ways than one. So where were you?"

"Working at the five and ten."

"Where's that?"

"On Third Avenue."

"What time did you leave work?"

"At five."

"Dom could have been killed any time between two and six. Where'd you go after work?"

"Home. To my apartment."

"Alone?"

"Laraine lives alone," Christine said. "Our parents are dead, and we're the only two children. We lived together until I got married."

"When was that?"

"Four years ago."

"What difference does it make?" Laraine said sharply. "Are you saying I shot Dom?"

"Did you?"

"Why would I?"

"This is ridiculous," Christine said.

"All right, let's skip it. I was leaving anyway. For Johnny's sake, you'd better not mention to the police that I was here. It won't help me, and it might hurt him."

"All right," Christine said.

"Nice meeting you," I said. "Both," I added, and I walked out of the apartment. I was going down the steps when I heard the voice behind me.

"Mr. Cordell!"

I stopped. I turned. Laraine was coming down after me. She walked with the swift sureness of a tall and pretty girl. She raised her straight black skirt as she came down the steps, dropping it when she reached me. She had long legs, and a tight skirt doesn't help with steep steps.

"What do you want?" I said.

"I want to apologize," she answered.

"What for?"

"For lacing into you."

"It's understandable," I told her. "Your brother-in-law was just killed. I imagine it upset you."

"Why should it?"

"Look, Laraine," I said, "I'm not your head-shrinker. It just seems natural to me that a girl would be upset when her sister's hus…"

"I'm not."

"Okay, let's leave it at that. We started off wrong together, and it isn't getting any better. Besides, I need a drink."

"I can use one, too," Laraine said.

"I didn't invite you."

"I'm inviting myself. Do you mind?"

"I thought I bothered you."

"I'm getting used to it." She took my arm. "I know a quiet bar. We can talk there."

"Maybe I ought to see a barber and a tailor first. Get spruced up."

"It wouldn't hurt," she said. She grinned. "But don't change a hair of you," she cracked. "I want to remember you this way always."

I laughed, and we headed for the bar.

Laraine's full name was Laraine Marsh. Her sister had been Christine Marsh. She was twenty-four years old, and she drank rye straight from a shot glass. Her eyes were very blue, and she never took them from a person's face, either while talking or listening. Mostly, she talked. We sat in a booth in a Third Avenue bar, and I told her straight off that I was a professional drinker who couldn't afford to pay for a social drinker's pleasure. She told me straight off that she would pay for the drinks this one time alone and so, understanding each other, we began to drink and talk.

I asked her if she liked her job.

"In the five and ten?" she said "What a drag that is!"

"Why don't you get another job?"

"There's only one job I want. And I'm going to get it some day."

"What's that?"

"Guess."

"Secretary to the president of General Motors."

"Nope."

"Miss Rheingold?"

"Nope."

"I don't like guessing games."

"The tradition is three guesses," Laraine said. "Take your last guess."

"High-priced call girl?"

Laraine laughed. "Is that what I look like?"

"That's not a bad thing to look like. They're the sleekest and best-dressed girls in New York."

"My ambitions aren't that lofty," she said.

"Okay, I've run out of guesses."

"I'm flattered, though. That you thought I could…"

"So what's your ambition?"

"…make the grade in what must be a highly competitive…"

"What's your ambition?"

"…field. I don't like to be interrupted, Cordell."

"Get friendly," I said. "Call me Matt. And go to hell."

"What?"

"I don't like women to tell me when to interrupt them."

"We get along fine, don't we?"

"Just dandy," I said. "I want another drink."

"Don't forget who's paying for it," Laraine said.

"I didn't ask for the free ride. I can pay for my own."

"It's my pleasure," she said.

"I think I know your ambition," I said.

"What?"

"You'd like to run a concentration camp."

"I'm a singer," Laraine said flatly.

"Are you?"

"And a damn good one."

I thought about this for a minute. Then I said, "How come such a good singer is working in the five and ten?"

"I'm waiting for the breaks," she told me.

"Well, I'm sure Cole Porter will come up to the East side for a spool of thread one day. He'll hear you humming behind the counter and sign you for his latest musical."

"I don't want to sing musical comedy."

"You've got the other necessary attributes for a musical comedy."

"I'm a popular singer. I sing with a band now."

"Anybody I know?"

"I doubt it. A bunch of local kids. We play weddings and beer parties, and like that. But it's work. And it's training."

"Sure," I said.

"There's a lot more to making the grade than just being good, you know."

"I didn't know."

"Sure. You need clothes and special arrangements,

and a good accompanist doesn't hurt, either. All that takes money. But I'll get there. I've got too much talent. Nothing's going to stop me."

"Well, good luck," I said.

"Thanks, but I don't need it. Luck is the one thing that doesn't play any part in this. All you need is talent and money. With that combination, you make your own breaks. You don't have to wait for Cole Porter to buy that spool of thread." She smiled. I smiled with her.

"You said Dom's death didn't upset you very much. How come?"

Laraine Marsh shrugged. Her body did very pretty things when she shrugged, but she seemed totally unaware of the chain reaction. She lifted her drink and sipped at it, and then wet her lips, or perhaps licked rye from them, it was difficult to tell. I felt good sitting opposite her. A pretty girl may not be like a melody, but she's certainly like a tonic, and Laraine Marsh was a pretty girl with something else. Maybe it was the drive. Maybe ambition boiled inside her and overflowed from her ears. Whatever it was, this girl bubbled with life. In Actor's Studio classes they'd have called her tense. Too tense, perhaps. But the tenseness provided a sort of electricity that bounded from the girl in engulfing bursts of brilliance. Sitting opposite her, feeling the life force, the electricity, the whatever the hell you want to call it, I began to like her. Nor was the liking purely intellectual. That life was bubbling inside a girl who was damned close to being beautiful. I've never been a person who was easily blinded by the bright lights. Doggedly, I tried my question again.

"Why weren't you upset to learn about Dom?"

"Dom was from Squaresville," she said, and I guess that summed it up.

"Didn't you like him?"

Again, Laraine shrugged. "You don't like or dislike a square," she said. "He just made no impression. He was my sister's husband. I saw them on holidays sometimes. Period. Do you mean was he the kind of brother-in-law who planted moist kisses on my cheeks and offered fatherly advice, no. He wasn't. He was, in many ways, a very cold and emotionless person."

"But your sister loved him," I said.

"Did she?"

"Didn't she?"

The table went silent for a moment. Theatrically, Laraine studied her shot glass and then killed what was left in it. She signaled for the waiter.

"Didn't she love him?" I repeated.

"Matt," she said, "I stopped analyzing people a long time ago. There isn't much percentage in it. I'm concerned with Number One right now, and that's me. I want to be a singer. I'm going to be a singer. I'm going to cut records and sell a million copies of each one. I'm going to make personal appearances, and I'm going to have my own network television show, and eventually I'm going to wind up in the movies where they can give me low-cut gowns designed by men in Paris. Me. Number One. Doris Day started as a singer, you know."

"I know."

"Okay. So it doesn't concern me what Christine felt for her husband. That's her business. If she wants to rant and rave after he's dead, fine. I'll go along with it. Why should I deny a widow her pleasure?"

"You sound as if you feel the grief was an act," I said.

"Is that the way I sounded? I'm sorry. I didn't mean to."

"Was it an act?"

"Judge for yourself. You're the detective. Christine and Dom haven't been living together for the past six months."

I digested this. The waiter came over to the table, and we ordered another round. Somebody at the back of the bar put a dime into the juke and Elvis Presley began pretending he had the lead in the musical version of *Blackboard Jungle*. Our drinks came. Laraine knocked hers off before you could say "Rumpelstiltskin." I nursed mine. I'm not a gentleman drinker, but I didn't want to leave the bar on my face.

"Why'd they separate?"

"She kicked him out."

"Why?"

"Did I say Dom was emotionless? He was. Except on one point, perhaps. Christine. I suppose he really loved her. Or at least he made wounded male animal noises in her presence. A very jealous man when it came to my sister. Couldn't even stand her *talking* to another man."

"*Was* there another man?"

"I doubt it. My sister looks deadly, but she learned her catechism well. The body was strictly for Dom."

"I see."

"Somebody spotless can get annoyed when she's constantly called unclean. If my sister ever entertained the thought of another man, she sure as hell never did anything about it. And it annoyed her that Dom constantly accused her. So she kicked him out."

"This was six months ago, you said?"

"Yes."

"And he hasn't been with her since?"

"No. In fact, he thought she kicked him out because there *was* another man. He even hired a detective to watch the place and report comings and goings."

"How do you know?"

"He told me."

"When?"

"I met him one day. About two months ago, I guess it was. He said he'd hired a detective to watch my sister."

"Wasn't that a little odd? Telling you, I mean."

"I don't carry tales," Laraine said flatly.

"Not even to your sister?"

"I keep my nose out of other people's business. That's why people tell me things. Dom knew he could tell me about the detective. In fact, he was probably dying to tell somebody."

"What was the detective's name?"

"Dennis something."

"Dennis Knowles?"

"Yes. Do you know him?"

"I know him," I said, but I made no further comment.

"Well, that's the guy."

"Is he still on the job?"

"I don't know," Laraine said. "That was the last time I saw Dom."

"Two months ago?"

"Yes. Understand this, Matt. I think Dom hired that man to prove to himself that he'd been wrong. I mean, it sounds peculiar, but he really loved Christine and wanted to learn for himself that she *didn't* have another man. Does that make any sense to you?"

"Yes, it sounds reasonable."

"Well, I don't know how reasonable it is, but that's the way I see it." She looked at her watch. "I've got to get out of here. Where are you going?"

"I've got a few ideas," I said.

"Like what?"

"I wanted to see your apartment."

Laraine looked at me quizzically. "Why?" she said.

"I'd like to go to bed with you."

She nodded. "Really?" she said.

"Yes. Really."

"That might be nice," she told me, "except for several items."

"Like what?"

"Like, for one, I have a very sensitive skin. I'm afraid the beard would be out of the question."

"I'll shave."

"That's nice of you," she said, "but there are other reasons."

"I'm still listening."

"I have a band rehearsal in ten minutes. Singing is a little more important to me than you are."

"I wouldn't think of interfering with your career," I said.

"You couldn't, believe me." She grinned. "But the third reason is the most important one."

"And what's that?"

"I don't want to go to bed with you, Matt Cordell."

"Why not?"

The smile dropped from her face. Her eyes got very serious. "Because I have a feeling I should stay away from you. Far away. I have that feeling."

"That's going to be difficult," I said. "I'm coming to your band rehearsal."

Chapter Four

You might say that I was digressing.

I was.

In later rationalization, I suppose I could claim that I knew the leader of the band in which Laraine Marsh sang was a kid named Dave Ryan who happened to be a part-time presser in Johnny's tailor shop. In truth, I did not know this when I offered to accompany Laraine to her rehearsal. I went with her because of a good many sound investigatory reasons, naturally. But the real reason I went with her was because she was a blonde who reminded me of Toni, and I was back where I had first met my ex-wife, and I wanted to be near this woman, and that was it. As a matter of fact, there weren't *any* investigatory considerations involved at all. I was digressing. I admit it. Shoot me.

The rehearsal was held in the basement of an apartment building on 116th Street, just off Third Avenue. The rain had washed the sidewalks and the asphalt, and water rushed in the gutters toward the sewers. It was only eight-thirty or so, still not dark, but a few lights had come on, and the sky westward was already washed with a soft duskiness. Laraine was a fast walker. She had long legs and a good stride, and I had trouble keeping up with her. She walked as if she knew exactly where she was going, and Christ help anyone who happened to step into her path.

"You'll find this very dull," she said. "Rehearsals always are. People come to rehearsals expecting a finished product, and they're always disappointed."

"I'll take my chances," I said.

The basement was in a building that housed a doctor's office on street level, and a dentist's office above that. I was wondering about how rehearsals sounded to a man being examined for cancer until we stepped into the room. There was, to be fair, the boiler in one corner, and the usual tenants' junk in another. But the ceiling pipes had been covered with acoustical tile, and the cement floor had been painted with grey paint, and there was a piano over against one wall, and the place looked very clean and neat. It wasn't Nola Studios, but it would do for a local bunch of musicians.

"The band fixed the room," Laraine explained. "That's why we get to rehearse here free. Come meet the boys." The boys, of which there were loosely seven or eight, had all glanced up when we came down the steps. They had been blowing their horns and warming up on snare and piano, and here I was; the horns stopped blowing and the piano stopped tinkling and the drummer sat up on his high wooden box with his sticks in mid-air. A fellow with a trumpet in his hands looked at Laraine inquiringly. In fact, there was more than inquiry in his brown eyes. There was something close to accusation.

"This is Matt Cordell," Laraine said to the assemblage. "A friend of mine."

The guy with the trumpet said, "I don't like outsiders at rehearsals, Laraine."

"That's too bad, Dave," she said. "He's a friend of mine."

He walked over to us. His walk was very hip, a sort of side-swinging walk, the trumpet dangling from his hand casually. He couldn't have been any older than twenty. He sported a Dizzy kick just beneath his lower lip, the beard allegedly designed to cushion a trumpet mouthpiece. His upper lip sported a white ring of muscle smack in the center, the badge of the trumpet player, the imprint of metal against flesh. He was a tall boy, with bright red hair and a narrow nose, the cheekbones of an Indian scout. Broad-shouldered, loose-hipped, he snaked his way across the room and said, "I'm Dave Ryan. I didn't mean to be rude, but I don't dig critics when we're blowing for free."

"You weren't rude," I said, "and I'm not a critic. But I'll leave if it makes you nervous."

"It don't make me nervous, Dad," Ryan said. "Pull up a chair. Don't applaud when we're good or boo when we're lousy. We'll get along fine."

"Are you the presser in Johnny Bridges' tailor shop?" I asked.

"Huh? Yeah. How'd you know?"

"Johnny mentioned your name."

"Oh yeah?" He studied me with careful brown eyes for a moment. Then he said, "The pressing buys sheet music. It's the horn I love." He was silent for a moment. "Anything else?"

"Nothing right now."

"Later?"

"If you feel like chatting."

"Right now, I feel like blowing. You mind?"

"Not at all."

"Gone. How's the throat, thrush?" he asked Laraine.

"It's fine."

"Want to take a swing at 'The Man'?"

"Sure," Laraine said.

Ryan turned to the other musicians. "Number fourteen," he said. "That mike set up, Frank?"

The piano player nodded and began fooling with the keyboard.

"All right, knock it off," Ryan said. "You set, Laraine?"

Laraine walked to the microphone, an old one that had seen far better days and that the boys had probably picked up at a radio studio fire clearance. She lowered the head, tightened the knob on the bar, and said, "I'm ready."

It's difficult to describe her voice exactly. She had an individual style that was Laraine Marsh, an immediate personal contact between singer and audience, no gimmicks, just a small emotional voice that sang the melody and sang it straight and managed to give it meaning. She wasn't imitating anyone, and she wasn't consciously striving for a unique style, but she did

have a unique style and its very ease revealed the
hours of practice that had gone into its development.

There was an audience of one in the room: me. And
perhaps that's why she fastened her eyes to my face
and didn't let go until the song was finished. But I had
the feeling that if there were a thousand men in that
small basement room, each and every one of them
would believe the song was being delivered to him
alone. If this girl vibrated across a table in a bar booth,
she positively throbbed when she sang. And then the
song ended, and she cut off the current by simply
closing her eyes for an instant. When she opened them
again, the music behind her had stopped.

I felt like applauding, but I remembered Ryan's
warning. I sat on my hands instead.

"Forty-seven," Ryan called off. " 'Lisbon Antigua.'
Rest your tonsils, Laraine. That was juicy."

Laraine walked over to where I was sitting. Ryan
called off the beat, and the band swung into motion.
"Did you like me?" she whispered.

"Very much."

"I get better," she said. "That was just a warmup.
Did you think I was singing to you?"

"Yes, I did."

"I was, in a way. But not really. It's a trick I learned
from the strippers in Union City. They make every
man in the audience think they're undressing just for
him alone."

"It's very effective. How's this Ryan kid? Any
good?"

"You heard him."

"I'm not an expert."

"Neither is he," Laraine said. "He'll probably get to be a big musician locally. Play all the weddings, all the picnics, play wherever they need a band. But he's not in my league, and he's not going where I'm going."

"Which is?"

"The top."

"Plenty of room up there, I understand."

"If there isn't, I'll make some," Laraine said, and she smiled. She lit a cigarette for herself and then belatedly offered me one. I took it. Ryan and the band struggled with "Lisbon Antigua" while we listened. They went at it for a good half-hour, and then he called a break and walked over to us.

"How did you like the band?" he said. He picked Laraine's purse from the chair, opened it, helped himself to a cigarette, and then closed it again. Laraine did not seem to mind what most other women might have considered an invasion of privacy.

"Am I allowed to comment?" I said.

"Sure."

"You sound pretty good," I told him. I wasn't lying. By the end of that half-hour, they had really whipped the arrangement into submission. They lacked the big-band sound, but they played with spirit and skill. Maybe they weren't going where Laraine was going—if indeed she was—but they were damned good for a bunch of local kids.

"You snowing me, or is this the goods?" he asked.

"It's from Straightsville," I said.

He smiled. "Gone." He paused, sucked in smoke, released it, and asked, "What's your dodge?"

"I'm a bum," I said.

"Yeah?"

"Yeah."

He looked to Laraine questioningly. Her face remained noncommittal. "I could teach you to press clothes," he said, half-seriously. "I'd teach you to blow trumpet, but that might take a little while."

"Neither profession seems to interest me," I said.

"Mr. Cordell is a detective," Laraine said suddenly, and Ryan turned to her sharply. He drew in on his cigarette, let out the smoke, and then turned back to me.

"Yeah? You don't look like a bull."

"I'm not."

"Private eye?" He smiled. "I thought they were only in books."

"I'm not a private eye, either. I used to be. I'm a bum now."

"Must be a good life," Ryan said.

"In the summer," I told him. "How long have you been playing trumpet?"

"Seven years. I'm still taking lessons."

"And the pressing?"

"Oh, that's just a fill-in job. Like I said, it pays for music. It ain't cheap, running a band."

"Well, how long have you worked for Johnny?"

"About three months, I guess," Ryan said. He looked

away from me, perhaps to cover the lie he'd just delivered. Or had Johnny been lying when he'd said Ryan had been working in the shop for six months?

"And you keep the job just to buy music, huh?"

"Sure," Ryan said. He turned to Laraine. "You want to sing a little more?" he asked.

"Whenever you say."

"I say now."

Laraine rose and squashed out her cigarette.

"I want to make a phone call," I said. "I'll be right back."

"Don't rush. We'll be here all afternoon."

"And then what?"

"Don't rush, Cordell," she repeated and walked to the microphone. The band started another tune and I climbed the steps. I found a drugstore with a phone booth, looked up Johnny's number, and called the tailor shop. I let the phone ring twelve times, and then hung up. I dialed the operator then and asked for the police. The sergeant at the local precinct identified himself, and I said, "Is there a man named Johnny Bridges there?"

"Who wants to know?"

"I do. I'm a friend of his."

"What's your name?" the desk sergeant asked.

"Joe Phillips," I lied.

"Just a second, Mr. Phillips. I'll check."

He cut himself off. I waited. Joe Phillips. That was a nice name. I pictured a cab driver who wore glasses. Joe Phillips.

"Detective Division, Andrews," a voice said.

"This is Mr. Phillips. I'm trying to locate a friend of mine named Johnny Bridges."

"He's here," Andrews said. "What's your interest, Mr. Phillips?"

"Personal," I said.

"So's ours," Andrews told me. "He's being held on suspicion of murder."

"Can I talk to him?"

"What for?"

"I'm a lawyer."

"Go chase another ambulance," Andrews said. "He's already phoned a lawyer."

"I see."

"Was there anything else, citizen?" Andrews asked.

I didn't answer him. I hung up, felt for my dime in the coin slot out of habit, and then walked out into the street. It was dark already, and the lights of the city nuzzled the warm summer night. On the East River, I could hear the sounds of the tugs, and from all over the city came the noise of horns and engines. I wanted a drink. I wanted Toni. Sometimes, it hit me like that, sometimes when the city became something more than steel and concrete, when it became a living breathing thing with a memory and a heart, it hit me. Suddenly it hit me, and I felt alone and lonely, and that was when I needed a drink most.

I put this one off.

I told myself that everything was working just the way I thought it would work. The police had picked up

Johnny, and he was now being grilled in the friendly atmosphere of the Detective Squad Room by cops who were already convinced he was a killer. He'd called a lawyer, and the lawyer would speak to Johnny, and tomorrow morning he would be taken down to the lineup because he was suspected of having committed a felony, and bulls from all over the city would examine him carefully, and then he would be arraigned, and bail might or might not be set while he waited trial. I hoped he'd got a good lawyer. I hoped he beat the rap. I hoped he got off scot free and went back to his little tailor shop. I needed a drink.

I stopped myself a second time because I knew what all that hoping amounted to. It amounted to leaving the guy in the hands of the law and a lawyer while I backed out. It amounted to breaking a bargain. I needed a drink, but Johnny needed a missing killer. I cursed myself for having gotten into this, and I cursed myself for being a coward, and I cursed myself for being a drunk and an idiot, but I didn't go into the nearest bar. I let the city press down on me with all its night noises and all its memories of Toni laughing to the night, and then I headed back for the basement and the band rehearsal. I pulled up a chair and listened to the sounds. The rehearsal broke up an hour later.

"Where to?" I asked Laraine.

"Back to my apartment," she said. She paused. "Where are *you* going?" she added pointedly.

I shrugged. "Got a razor there?"

"Yes."

"Whose?"

"Do you want a shave or a pedigree?"

"I'll settle for the shave."

"Matt…," she said.

"Yes?"

"I don't…I don't want to get involved with you."

"Why not?"

She shook her head.

"Why not?" I repeated.

"I don't think you can take it if I give it to you straight."

"Try me."

"Okay. I'm not Toni McAllister. If you think I am, you're crazy. I'm Laraine Marsh. And I don't want salty tears for her on my bosom."

"That's straight enough," I said.

"So let's call it a day." She held out her hand. "If I can help you in any way, with this thing about Dom, just let…"

"I still need a shave," I said. "I'd also like to make a phone call. Do you have a phone?"

"Yes."

"May I?"

Laraine sighed. "Come on," she said.

The phone call I wanted to make was to a private detective named Dennis Knowles. I probably would have made my call, taken my shave, and then been kicked out of the apartment by Laraine were it not for what happened downstairs in the hallway.

I wanted to call Knowles because it seemed to me the presence of a private detective on the scene might indicate there was more to Dom's suspicion about his wife than Laraine was willing to admit. And if Christine *did* have a lover, he was an ideal candidate for the man who'd put two holes in Dom's chest. Knowles was a very live man with a very hot practice. He always got results. You wanted a divorce? Dennis Knowles was your man. If your husband didn't happen to be playing around with another woman, Dennis would supply one. He would also supply a strong shoulder with which to collapse a hotel door, a camera with which to snap the couple in a somewhat compromising attitude, and a few witnesses to swear to the validity of the scene.

A nice fellow, Dennis Knowles, a fellow spawned by a system that refused divorce except on grounds of adultery or desertion. Dennis was a whole hell of a lot cheaper than six weeks in Reno. But whereas I didn't like him or his practices, I wanted to find out more about why Dom had hired him. This seemed to me an essential part of the case. At the same time, I really did want a shave, and I was hoping that Laraine Marsh might see in me a little more than a bum once the whiskers were gone. She might not have, though, if it weren't for what happened in the hallway.

We went into the building together. Her apartment was on the third floor. I don't know if you've ever been inside an East Side tenement, but they stink. You can do whatever you want inside your own apartment, decorate it as if you lived on Sutton Place, but the building stinks, figuratively and literally. The mailboxes are usually broken, and the entrance hallway is as dark as a satchelful of eight balls, and the hallways and the stairs all the way up to the roof are usually as dim as life through a cataract eye. We started up the steps, and when we reached the second floor landing, Laraine said, "I forgot to pick up my mail."

She fished into her purse for the key, and I held out my hand.

"I'll go down for it," I said.

"Thank you."

Laraine leaned on the bannister while I went down the steps. I was unlocking her mailbox when I heard the scream from upstairs. And then the scream stopped suddenly as if someone had clamped a hand over her mouth. I took the steps up two at a time.

Muggers are not uncommon in this section, and this mugger was as big as life, his hand over Laraine's mouth, his free fingers clutching for the purse she carried. I reached the landing, and he released her the moment he saw me. He drew back his fist and threw it forward at my head and Laraine screamed again as I backed off against the bannister, waiting for his blow. I threw up an elementary Judo block, my arm stiff, and then I clutched the material of his sleeve in my left hand, and I thrust my right hand out to grab the cloth on the right hand side of his shirt. Judo, contrary to popular belief, isn't all a science of wrestling holds. If a man is wearing clothes, you make use of them.

He was slightly off balance anyway, having just swung with his right fist. I pulled him further off balance with the grip I had on his shirt, and then I swung my right foot just behind and a little below the calf of his right leg, and I kicked and pulled simultaneously and he swung sideways and started to fall. It was a simple throw. In the gym, I'd have held tight to my opponent's sleeve, breaking his fall even though he was trained to fall properly. This was not the gym, nor was the mugger trained to fall, nor did I hold onto his sleeve. I slammed him down, and he landed on his wrist, hurting it but not breaking it, and then his back collided with the wooden floor, and he was sprawled across the tips of my shoes with me leaning over him. I brought up my left hand and sent the hard edge of it down across the bridge of his nose. If I'd hit him harder, I'd have sent bone splinters into his brain, killing him instantly. I didn't hit him that hard. I only wanted to stun him, and stun him I did. He blinked and shook his head and then tried to get to his feet, and I hit him again, on the right shoulder this time, very hard, and he fell back against the floor unable to move his right arm.

I grabbed the back of his shirt and pulled him off the floor and then shoved him down the steps in front of me. I threw him out into the street and then hurried back upstairs to where Laraine was trembling against the bannister.

"It's all right," I said.

"Matt...Matt..."

"It's all right."

"He just came from...from..."

"Where's your key?" I said.

I helped her upstairs and opened the door for her. I flicked on the lights. It was a nice apartment, tastefully furnished. There was a police lock on the inside of the kitchen door. I put it in place, the bar leaning against the door to form a triangle with the heavy steel plate embedded in the floor. Then I found the liquor and poured two stiff shots for both of us. Laraine accepted hers gratefully.

"Thank you," she said.

"For the whiskey?"

"For what you did out there."

"You're welcome."

"Did you call a cop?"

"No. I'm trying to keep away from them."

"Do you think he'll come back?"

"If he does, there won't be a third time."

"Thank you," she said again.

We stared at each other foolishly for a few minutes.

"I'll make my phone call," I said.

"The phone's there." She pointed to a small table at the end of the sofa. I looked up Knowles' number and dialed it. No one answered. The office was apparently closed for the night. I checked the book again, but a home phone was not listed.

"No luck," I said. "Do I still get the shave?"

"The razor's in the bathroom," she said. "Second

shelf of the medicine chest. I use it for my legs. I don't know if there are any unused blades."

"I'll manage," I said. "And I'll clear out right after I finish."

She got out of the chair and she came to me, and she put her arms around my neck, and she kissed me as soundly as I've been kissed in my life.

Then she said, "No. No, you will not get out." She kissed me again, and I pulled her to me, and she turned her head aside with a little whimpering sound, and she said, "Oh, you bastard, why are you letting this happen?"

Chapter Five

Knowles Investigations was on Fifty-third Street, directly opposite the Museum of Modern Art. The building was a converted brownstone that housed a private gallery on street level, a photographer's agent on the first floor, a place that sold African *objets d'art* on the second floor, and Dennis' establishment on the top floor.

I arrived there at ten a.m. on Wednesday morning. Laraine had washed and ironed my shirt and pressed my suit. I looked fairly decent. I felt pretty good, too. I don't know how much Laraine had to do with that, but I imagined it was a great deal. We'd had breakfast together that morning before she left for the five and ten. She'd sat opposite me in a bra and half-slip, and we'd drunk orange juice and coffee, and this had been the first morning in a long while that I hadn't started the day with a belt from a bottle. We talked while she dressed. I told her I would probably be busy downtown all day, and she made me promise to eat lunch someplace. She also insisted that I return to the apartment by six o'clock. She would have dinner waiting, she said. I helped her zip up the back of her dress. I always suspect this to be a feminine trick designed to make a man feel more masculine. There are, after all, countless American females who live alone, and they don't run around with the zippers lowered at the backs of their dresses. They are, *ipso facto,* capable of doing the zipping themselves. But feminine trick or not, I enjoyed it. Laraine kissed me before she left the apartment. I enjoyed that, too. I had a second cup of coffee, and then headed downtown for Knowles' office.

A couple of young farm girls with hayseed sticking out of their ears were waiting outside the photographer's agent's door. They looked up at me hopefully when I came up the steps, and then turned away disdainfully when I plowed on past. A big African mask decorated the door on the third floor. It scared hell out of me.

Knowles had a very nice office on the top floor. The business of breaking down hotel doors had apparently been thriving since last I'd seen him. I entered a cozy reception room with a cozy brunette receptionist, and I walked to her desk and said, "I'd like to see Mr. Knowles, please."

The brunette looked up from her emery board. "Who's calling, please, sir?"

I debated the advisability of using my own name. Dennis and I had never seen eye-to-eye even when things were going good for me. If he heard Matt Cordell was here, he'd probably come out of his office raging. I decided to reactivate my old cab-driver friend.

"Joe Phillips," I said.

"Won't you have a chair, Mr. Phillips," the brunette said. "I'll see if Mr. Knowles is free."

I had a chair, and she had a conversation on the telephone. When she put the receiver back onto the cradle, she said, "Go right in, won't you?"

I opened the door to the private office, closed it quickly behind me, and then leaned on it. Knowles looked up, registered little if any shock, smiled, and said, "Joe Phillips, huh?"

"Hello, Dennis," I said.

He was sitting behind his desk, a big man in a lightweight sports jacket. By big, I mean six-two and about 200 pounds, which is not unusual for a detective. Most detectives I know are tall and heavy, and Knowles was no exception. His broad shoulders were silhouetted by the bank of windows behind him. There was a small terrace outside the windows, fronting on Fifty-third. I wondered if he went out there to meditate on how best to splinter a door. He studied me now with a slight smile still on his face. He had good teeth, and a strong jaw. His brown eyes were shrewdly intelligent. His nose had once been broken in a fist-fight. I happen to know this because I'm the guy who broke it.

"Sit down, Matt," he said, and I instantly suspected him. I took the leather-covered chair alongside his desk. Knowles offered me a cigar from the humidor on his desk. I took it, but I didn't light it. I stuck it in the breast pocket of my jacket instead.

"You're looking good, Dennis," I said.

"Thanks." He lit his cigar, filling the office with smoke. "What's on your mind, Matt?"

"Just like that?"

"What would you rather discuss? My nose?" he grinned.

"The slight hook gives you character," I said.

"Thanks. Such character I could have done without." He paused. "I never thought I'd see you again. Am I supposed to apologize for having insulted your wife that time?"

"The way I figure it, the broken nose makes us even."

"The way I figure it," Knowles said, "the only thing that makes a broken nose even is another broken nose."

"Meaning, Dennis?"

"Meaning let's stop playing footsie. What the hell do you want in my office?"

"Ahhh," I said, "there's that old Dennis Knowles fire."

"I'm a busy man," Knowles said. "If you came here to chat, I'm not a big talker. If you came for a handout, business is bad. If you came for another swing at my nose, I wouldn't try it again. What's on your mind?"

"A woman named Christine Archese," I said.

"What about her?"

"Are you tailing her?"

"Goodbye, Matt," Knowles said, and he rose and slammed the lid of his humidor shut. He looked bigger standing—but not that big.

"I asked a civil question, Dennis."

"What gives you the right to ask?"

"Haven't you seen the morning papers?" I said.

"I never read the papers," Knowles answered. "They make me nervous."

"Dom Archese was shot dead yesterday."

Knowles sat down. He wasn't shocked or anything. I guess he was just tired. He sat down, flicked ash from his cigar, puffed on it again, and uninterestedly said, "Yeah?"

"Twice in the chest. At his tailor shop. Was Christine playing around?"

"What's your interest?"

"A friend of mine may be involved."

"You practicing again?"

"No. I'm doing a favor for a friend."

"The Good Samaritan," Knowles said. "There's such a thing as protecting the confidences of a client, Matt. You know that as well as I do. You've also got a hell of a lot of gall, if you don't mind my saying so. The last time I see you, you break my nose for mentioning what's in all the goddamn newspapers anyway. Now you come around and ask me to betray a client's confidence."

"Your client is dead, Dennis," I said.

"What the hell are you talking about?"

"Didn't you hear me? Dom Archese was shot yesterday."

"Archese isn't and wasn't my client," Knowles said.

I looked at him and blinked. He didn't blink back.

"Okay," I said. "If you won't help me…"

"I'm telling you the truth, Christ knows why," Knowles said. "You sure as hell don't deserve it. But you're the only bastard who ever threw a punch at me and didn't get sent to the hospital. I respect fists. I'm not afraid of you, but I respect you. I hope you understand the difference."

"I understand it." I paused. "Archese wasn't your client?"

"No."

"Who is?"

"I'm afraid I can't tell you that."

I sighed and wiped a hand over my jaw. "Look, Dennis, a friend of mine is in pretty serious trouble. Archese was his partner."

"His *partner*!" Knowles said.

"Yes. What…"

"Your friend isn't Johnny Bridges, is he?"

"Yes, how did you know?"

"Well, for Christ's sake, *he's* my client!"

The room went very still. Dennis sucked in smoke. I scratched my head.

"Johnny?"

"Yes, yes, Johnny."

"Your client?"

"My client."

"Why?"

"Oh, what the hell's the sense in keeping anything from you?" Knowles said. "He came to me about three months back. Walked into the office and said, 'My name is Johnny Bridges. I'd like you to do some work for me.'"

"What kind of work? Cash register thefts? Was that it?"

"No, no, why the hell would I get involved in something like that? You know the kind of work I do. Well, that's the kind of work he wanted."

"But Johnny isn't married," I said.

"I know he isn't. Look, are you sure he's a friend of yours?"

"Yes. I'm sure."

"I'll check the next time he calls, you know."

"He isn't going to be calling, Dennis. The police have him."

"That's great," Knowles said. "He still owes me money."

"What did you do for him, Dennis?"

"He's in love," Knowles said. "With a blonde."

"Named?"

"Christine Archese."

I was beginning to get puzzled. I admit it. None of this tied in with what I already knew. Either Dennis was lying or a lot of people before him had lied. Or maybe it had been too long since I'd had a shot of whiskey.

"Let me get this straight," I said. "Johnny Bridges, according to you, is in love with Christine Archese."

"That's what the man said. That's why he hired me."

"To do what? Write love poems?"

"No. To get the goods on Dom Archese."

"Oh, come on, Dennis! What the hell are you giving me?"

"Do you want it or not?" Knowles said.

"I want it."

"Okay, so shut up. I'll tell you what one of your biggest faults is, Matt. You don't listen. A good investigator knows when to shut up."

I shut up. Knowles nodded, sucked in on his cigar, and said, "Apparently this Dom Archese knew all about the big torrid love affair and refused to give Christine a divorce. About six months ago, to show him she meant business, she kicked him out of the apartment. He still wouldn't come across. Johnny and Christine sat it out for a while, hoping he'd change his mind. About three months ago, they decided he'd never change his mind. Johnny came to me, determined to do something about it."

"What did he hope to do?"

"He was working on the assumption that everyone has a skeleton in his closet. Archese had been separated from his wife for three months. Was it not reasonable to assume he might have started something with another frail during that time? Johnny wanted me to find out."

"And if you found out Archese *wasn't* playing around?"

Knowles shrugged.

"You'd rig a scene?" I asked.

"I hadn't suggested that to my client. I doubt if it would have been necessary."

"You mean Archese *was* playing around?"

"There were indications of that, yes," Knowles said.

"I don't believe you," I said flatly.

"I never make mistakes," Knowles said. "Bridges gave me a picture of Archese, and he gave me his address. Archese was living alone, so there were no mistakes. We followed the right man, and we were building a good case against him. Now you tell me he's dead."

"That's right."

"And Johnny is involved in it."

"Sort of. His initials were written on the wall. Allegedly by the dead man."

"Ouch!" Knowles said. He paused, thinking. "What kind of a guy is this Johnny Bridges?" he asked.

"Don't you know? He's your client."

"Yeah, but he was always very mysterious. You know how some of them get. Embarrassed because they're dealing with a detective. He wouldn't even give me his address or phone number. Paid me a retainer in advance and then came in every week like clockwork to pay me for the past week's work. He still owes me for last week. You think they'll let him out on bail?"

"I hope so."

"I hope so, too. I need that money. He usually calls me two, three times a week. If they let him out, I guess he'll call, huh?"

"I guess so."

I wanted a drink. I was very mixed up. Nothing seemed right anymore. I was beginning to think, if what Knowles said was true, that maybe Johnny Bridges *had* shot Archese. Maybe those initials on the wall really did point to the killer. In which case everyone but Knowles was lying. Johnny was lying, and Christine was lying, and even Laraine was lying. It didn't make sense.

"Did you work on this one personally, Dennis?" I said.

"No."

"Who did?"

"One of my people. A girl named Fran West."

"A girl?"

"Um-huh. A trick I learned. Put a female tail on a guy and he never tips that he's being followed. I guess guys are naturally more suspicious of other guys, huh?"

"I guess so. One question, Dennis."

"Shoot. And then get the hell out. I'm busier'n hell."

"Have you been telling me the truth?"

Dennis Knowles smiled crookedly. "Now, Matt," he said, "would I lie to you?"

I went downstairs past the African mask, past the country girls waiting and anxious to have their pictures taken nude for the cheese magazines, and then past the private gallery on the ground floor, the oils by an unknown Mexican artist decorating the window facing the street. It was only eleven o'clock but the sun had already turned on its wattage and the sidewalks were steaming. It was going to be another scorcher, and the pale blue sky held no promise of rain-relief. I loosened my tie and walked into the museum.

I don't like to be puzzled. I think that's why I became a detective in the first place. Puzzles bother me. I was always good in math in high school, mainly because I refused to become puzzled by the puzzle. I'd fit the pieces together until I got the right answer, and then I'd check the answer, and with mathematics it always worked. Life isn't quite like math, but if you add two and two, you usually get four. I was adding two and two now and coming up with five. Or seven. Or nine. But never four. I kept trying to figure everyone's stake in this thing, and the possible reasons for the possible lies. Nobody lies unless he feels he has to. Then why were all these people lying?

I needed a drink, but I settled for a cup of coffee from the museum's shop. I went outside to drink it, sitting among the huge statues in the garden. It was very peaceful and relaxing there. Toni and I used to go to the outdoor garden often. If you want serenity in the midst of the busiest city in the world, that's the place to find it. I found it that Wednesday morning, sipping at my coffee.

If Dennis Knowles had told me the truth, everyone else was lying—either by commission or omission.

Johnny had allegedly sought me to help him with some petty cash register pilfering. He'd never once mentioned that he was in love with Christine Archese or that he and she were trying to obtain a divorce from Dom. Nor had he mentioned going to Dennis Knowles for help.

Christine, when she'd learned of her husband's death, had carried on like an Indian squaw ready to roll in the ashes. If she truly loved Johnny, if she were truly bucking for divorce, her hysterics had all been an act, a lie. Laraine had told me that Dom hired Knowles to watch his wife Christine. And Knowles had just told me it was Johnny Bridges who'd hired him.

Unless Knowles was lying...

This was a possibility. He'd taken the broken nose like a true sport, and I suspected his good fellowship. A man who breaks down doors for a living isn't exactly the kind of man who'll easily forget a ruptured proboscis. But at the same time, he'd sounded honest and sincere when he'd professed his respect for me. And I'd known many a louse who, contradictorily, held high ideals and standards in a very personal narrow area of emotion or thought.

Why the hell *should* he lie to me?

The nose. All right, maybe he did harbor a grudge over the nose and was enjoying a private revenge by screwing me up with a completely crazy story. That was possible.

On the other hand, he knew I wasn't getting paid for my legwork, and the only person who'd suffer from his misinformation would be Johnny Bridges whom I was trying to help. If Johnny hadn't hired Knowles, he had no reason for wanting to injure a perfect stranger. And if he had, he certainly wouldn't want to foul up a client who still owed him money.

There was a faint breeze in the garden. The breeze found the open throat of my shirt, lingered there like a warm caress. I sipped at my coffee, and I kept my mind away from other times in this same garden, but it was impossible to shut out the thoughts, impossible to squelch the picture of Toni that managed to sneak in wherever I went, whatever I did.

I put down the coffee cup.

I got off the bench and walked back into the museum. I didn't much feel like working right then, but I also didn't feel like being puzzled. Knowles had said a girl named Fran West worked on the case. If he'd been lying to me, she'd know it. Provided she was willing to talk about it. Provided Dennis hadn't already reached her and filled her in on the lie. Provided she was listed in the phone book. Provided she was home.

I found a listing for Francine West on West 10th Street in the Village. I waited while a fat woman in the phone booth spoke to a Mr. Arbiter about the Roualt print she'd bought and would it go in the living room over the chartreuse sofa?

"But it has a *lot* of colors," she insisted, in answer to something he said. "Well, of course there's some chartreuse in it. Would I have bought it if there weren't any chartreuse in it?"

I waited.

Eventually, the woman and Mr. Arbiter both seemed satisfied. She came out of the booth, smiled and said, "My God, it's hot, isn't it?"

I nodded. The smell of her perfume was still in the booth. I left the door open, deposited a dime and dialed Fran West's number. A phone call can often save a very long journey. I let the phone ring four times. It was answered just as the fifth ring started.

"Yes?" the woman said.

"Miss West?"

"Yes?"

I hung up and headed west.

Chapter Six

I like Greenwich Village.

It's close to home, home being the Bowery, and maybe that's why I feel comfortable there. It's got a large quota of phonies, but it's also got some of the liveliest and most devoted people in the city. And if you cut your way through the deviates and the fakes starving in attics because they want to pretend they're artists, you'll find people of talent and grace, and there's little enough of that in the world today. You'll also find a lot of ordinary working stiffs who commute to jobs in midtown Manhattan every day and who live in the Village because they like this feeling of a small town within a big town. The Village is gaudy sometimes, and sometimes it's violent, and sometimes the things you see there can make you want to vomit. But most of the time it's just a place where people live, and most people are all right.

Fran West's street was quiet and hot. The building in which she lived had air-conditioners sticking out of one window on each floor, and I thanked God and hoped hers would be working. An old man was sweeping the front steps when I came up. He stepped into my path and rested one hand on the broom as if he were handling a rifle.

"Who you looking for?" he said.

"Francine West," I told him.

"Third floor," he said. "You a friend of hers?"

"Business associate."

"I own this building," the old man said. "I don't go for shenanigans. You got business with Miss West, you get it done fast and come down fast. Else, I'll be up."

"You had me fooled for a minute," I said.

"Huh?"

"You shaved off the mustache, didn't you?"

"Huh?"

"Don't worry. I won't tell anyone you're still alive."

"Huh?"

"Or where you're hiding, Adolph."

I left him on the front step scratching his head. I pressed the buzzer for Francine West, apartment 3C, and then opened the inner door when she answered my ring. The lobby of the building had been knocked down and done over with a huge glass panel facing the street. But inside the entrance doorway, the original wooden bannister swooped upward with the original rickety steps. I took the steps leisurely. On the third floor, I looked for 3C, found it, and pressed my thumb to the ivory stud set in the door jamb.

From behind the door, a voice said, "Who is it?"

"Matt Cordell," I answered.

There was a pause. "I don't know you."

"Dennis Knowles sent me."

"How do I know?"

"You don't. Open the door and take a chance. Daylight rapes are very uncommon."

Behind the door, Fran West stifled a laugh. I heard the bolt being thrown, and then the door opened a crack, held by the night chain. In the crack, Fran West said, "What do you want, Mr...."

"Cordell. I want to talk to you about Dom Archese."

"What about him?"

"Won't it be easier inside?"

"It's pretty easy the way it is," Fran said.

"Your neighbors might overhear us. This is pretty confidential."

"I've only got one neighbor and he leaves for work at six-thirty in the morning."

"Dennis won't like the way you're treating a new member of the firm," I said.

"Are you working for Dennis?"

"Yes."

"Since when?"

"Since this morning."

"Then you won't mind if I call him to check, will you?"

"Not at all."

"Your name is Cordell?"

"Matt Cordell, that's right. If you're going to call him, please hurry, will you? I don't like standing in hallways."

Fran thought about it for a moment. Then she said, "You sound okay," and she took the chain off the door. It was thirty degrees cooler inside. I felt the chill instantly and almost shuddered. Fran didn't seem to mind the cold. She was wearing a black sweater and black slacks, tapered to hug her ankles. She wore black slippers, and her hair was as black as her costume, blacker, the richest blackest hair I'd ever seen on a woman. Her eyes were brown, and she wore no makeup, no powder, no lipstick, so that the wide brown eyes became the focal point of what was essentially a plain face.

"Come on in the living room," she said, and I followed her into a room with a fireplace on one wall and yellow nylon drapes on another. Dramatically, she went to stand by the draped wall instantly, a black shadow against the bright lemon yellow. "Sit down."

"Thank you." I sat. A cigarette box was on the table, so I lifted the lid and had one.

"What about Archese?" she said.

"He's dead."

"Killed or dropped?"

"He was shot."

"That's nice," Fran said. She walked to the table and speared a cigarette for herself. Gallantly, I lighted it. She blew smoke at me and asked, "When did this happen?"

"Yesterday afternoon."

"I guess I should have the morning papers deliv-

ered," she said. "I'm a late sleeper. By the time I get
the news, it happened four days ago. How'd you get
into this?"

"Dennis hired me. I used to work with him a long
time ago," I lied.

"What's the matter? Didn't he like the job I was
doing?"

"He liked it fine. But murder complicates it a little.
He feels a man ought to be around now."

"Why?" she said, and it was a damn good question
because I know of very few private investigators who
will mess around with murder. The minute a homicide
intrudes into a case, the private eye will pick up his fee
and steal into the desert night.

"Johnny Bridges is involved," I said. "He's still the
agency's client until he notifies us otherwise. We may
be able to save him a lot of trouble if we can establish
where he was, what he was doing…"

"Cut the gobbledegook," Fran said, "and tell me
why Dennis thought he had to bring in somebody else
on this."

"He's worried about you," I said in a final stab.

"Ha!"

"He is. With a murderer running around, who can
tell?" I shrugged in what I hoped was a realistically
concerned manner.

"The day Dennis Knowles starts worrying about
anyone but himself is the day I'll run out to buy a
padded bra," Fran said. The image was not wasted on
me. The girl's bosom was high and full beneath the

black sweater, a natural softness crowding the wool, a softness foam rubber could never hope to achieve.

"You have a point," I said, "but Dennis hired me anyway, and since we're all in the same boat now, couldn't we drop the suspicion and get down to brass tacks?"

Fran shrugged. "There's only one brass tack, and it looks like I just sat on it. Dennis is dissatisfied with my work."

"That's not so," I said. "Nor is it uncommon for more than one person to work on the same case. You should know that. How long have you been doing investigation work?"

"Not too long."

"How long?"

"This is my first case, really. A promotion, sort of. Before this, I was doing...modeling."

"Oh." She didn't have to elaborate. Dennis had been using her as one of his professional correspondents. Fran West was one of the ladies who, fairly undraped, had their pictures taken in bed when the door was shattered. I visualized her fairly undraped. The picture was convincing. There was nothing professional looking about her, no hardness, no slick painted exterior. She looked like a nice girl—and maybe she was.

"I can see the wheels clicking," she said. "You're drawing the wrong conclusions."

"Am I?"

"Insufficient evidence," she said, and she smiled.

"An investigator should never build a case on piece-meal facts, unquote. A gem of wisdom from the great man himself."

"Dennis?"

"Dennis. To set you straight, Mr. Cordell, I did professional modeling. I hesitated on the word because most people think of fashion models when the word 'modeling' is mentioned. I'd be a little incongruous as a fashion model. To model clothes, you need an exquisitely boned face, no bosom, a boy's hips, and long thin legs. I'm plain as mud, and I run to fat. I couldn't model a chemise because I'd fill out the damn thing."

"What kind of modeling *did* you do?"

"Cheesecake." She paused. "You don't need an Egyptian goddess face for cheesecake. Nobody looks at the faces in a cheesecake magazine."

"Why'd you leave modeling?"

"I went into a secondhand magazine shop once, and I saw the kind of men who buy the girlie mags. I decided to make an honest woman of myself. I'm very strong. I took a course in Judo, and then I applied for a job with the city police. I failed the written examination. I guess I'm pretty stupid. Anyway, I finally got a job with Dennis. Actually, I'd probably be a decoy for subway mashers if I was a lady cop. This way, I really get to do some investigation."

"Which brings us to Johnny Bridges."

"If you like." She shrugged. "Can I get you a drink or something?"

"I'd like a drink fine."

She went into the kitchen and came back with a fifth of bourbon. "I never drink before three in the afternoon," she said. "A standing rule of mine. Bourbon all right?"

"Bourbon's fine. What are your other standing rules?"

"They'd bore you. Besides, you want to talk about Johnny Bridges, don't you?"

"It's rare that I get the occasion to drink socially with a nice girl."

"Why, thank you."

"And the rules?"

"Rule one: never touch a drink before three in the afternoon. Rule two: never wear a girdle. Rule three: never invite a man up for a nightcap unless I plan to let him stay the night. Rule four: be a lady. Rule five: except when it's impossible."

I laughed. Fran laughed with me.

"That's a good set of rules," I said, still laughing. I was beginning to like her very much. There was honesty and freshness about her. Freshness is a thing cultivated by women who, once all the gook is washed away, are about as fresh as the Roman Senate. And because it is a cultivated look and attitude, it loses all semblance of freshness. Fran was truly fresh. Honesty is something you can't cultivate. You're either honest or you're not. And she was. Or at least I thought so.

"What are your rules?" she said, and she handed me the bourbon. "Or do you have any?"

"I have some."

"You have to have five. If you don't, they're not really rules, they're only daily reminders."

"Rule number one," I said, "take a drink whenever it's offered, regardless of the time of day. Rule two: never wear a girdle. Rule three: never call a proposition a nightcap. Rule four: always recognize a lady. Rule five: except where it's impossible."

"Am I recognizable?" Fran asked.

"You are indeed."

"Thank you again. I think there may be a poet under that Brooks Brothers suit."

I laughed again, this time at my own expense. The suit I was wearing was as close to being Brooks Brothers as I was close to being Adolph Menjou. "I haven't laughed this way in a long time," I said.

"Good. People should laugh, don't you think? There's too much seriousness in the world. Maybe I will have a drink after all."

"Rule number six," I said. "Never break rules one to five."

Fran smiled. "And rule number seven: never mix business with pleasure. Shall we talk about Johnny Bridges?"

"If you like."

"I'd rather talk about drinking or laughing, but Dennis isn't paying us for that, is he?"

"No, he's not."

"Okay. Johnny Bridges. I was in the office when he came in that day. Said he was in love with a married woman whose husband refused to give her a divorce. Wanted us to follow the man until we got something on him."

"The man was Dom Archese."

"Right."

"You followed him?"

"I did. Every day."

"Did you get anything on him?"

"Plenty."

"Like?"

"Like a little blonde he was seeing a great deal of. Met her regularly."

"A blonde? Who?"

"A girl named Laraine Marsh."

I took a gulp at the bourbon. "Christine's sister? Dom was seeing *her*?"

"I didn't know she was Christine's sister," Fran said. "That complicates it a little, doesn't it?"

"More than you know. Are you sure Dom was seeing her?"

"Regularly. Once or twice a week."

"How cozy were they?"

"Hard to say. It looked legit, the usual Friday or Saturday night date stuff. But he also spent a lot of time in her apartment. We were going to put a tap on her phone, just to find out exactly how chummy they were. Now that Dom's dead..." Fran shrugged.

"Did you tell this to Bridges?"

"Yes."

"When?"

"Last week sometime. We suggested the wiretap, and he said he wanted to think it over. Truthfully, he seemed to be losing his enthusiasm for the whole project. I can't understand why. He wanted Dom to divorce Christine, and we were working in that direction. But he didn't seem too impressed with what we'd told him. Maybe he was falling *out* of love. It's possible."

"And sometimes easier than falling *in* love."

"Sometimes," Fran said.

"Well, I don't know what to think," I said honestly. "You're sure Dom Archese was seeing a lot of Laraine Marsh?"

"Positive."

"And you didn't know she was Christine's sister?"

"No. I guess I goofed, huh? She went to the apartment several times, but I figured it was to see Dom. A nice sister to have, huh?"

"Very nice."

"Do you know her?"

"Yes, I know her."

"Would you call her a lady?"

"Insufficient evidence," I said, smiling. "An investigator should never build a case on piecemeal facts, unquote."

"The way the police built their case against you?" Fran asked, unsmiling.

"Huh?"

"It clicked a little while back. I read about you in the papers."

"Okay," I said.

"I don't think you're working for Dennis," Fran said.

"No?"

"No. He once told me about a guy who broke his nose. Seems to me your name came up."

"That's entirely likely."

"Who *are* you working for?"

"I'm not really working. I'm simply trying to help someone."

"You're an appealing guy, Matt. I'll tell you why. Would you like to know why?"

"Sure."

"Every woman in the world knows you took a beating from a beautiful and exciting woman. God, the papers had a field day with her pictures, didn't they?"

"Yes," I said tiredly.

"All right, it still hurts you to talk about it. Shall we stop?"

"I'd rather."

"I'd rather not," Fran said, "and this all ties in with what is your basic appeal to women everywhere. You're a man who's been hurt, and by a beautiful gal. Aside from the natural instinct of wanting to mother you, there's also the challenge. It's a challenge no real woman can ignore. It's a challenge to her competitive spirit and her femaleness and her survival pattern. Do you know what the challenge is?"

"What?" I said.

"The challenge is whether or not she can make you forget…what was her name?"

"Toni."

"Toni McAllister. Right. The challenge is whether she can put out the torch, whether her arms, her body, her lips, will make you forget a woman who—to you— was the most…"

"Let's drop it," I said.

"Your reluctance enhances the challenge," Fran said. "You're a very appealing guy, Matt."

"And you're a very unflattering gal," I told her. "I don't like to think of myself as forbidden fruit that will nurture the ego of a dame with an inferiority complex."

"Inferiority has nothing to do with it. Hell, the battle is a daily one. It even goes on between daughters and their own mothers. You don't know very much about women."

"I guess not."

"You can learn," she said. "I could teach you. I'm a pretty smart girl."

"There's just one thing I'd like to know," I said.

"Mmm?"

"How come you failed that police examination?"

Fran smiled, and then allowed the smile to become a laugh. "You threw down your gauntlet to every woman in the world the day you beat up that jerk and allowed yourself to be destroyed by something that happens every day everywhere. And you can't blame women for wanting to pick it up."

"Are you picking up the gauntlet, Fran?"

"I'd like to, if you'd let me. Getting you to forget

that bitch would be the most creative thing any woman could do."

"Have you tried having a baby?" I said.

"Only once," she answered honestly and soberly. "It didn't work out." She paused. "I'm not the original laughing girl, Matt. I've had it, too, in spades." She paused again. "I know how to love. I love very deeply when I do."

"Good."

"And the gauntlet is still on the ground."

"We'll pick it up some time," I said.

With complete honesty, Fran West said, *"When?"*

"Not tonight, Josephine."

She laughed. "Perhaps I should add that I also think you're a hell of a nice guy. Or is that necessary?"

"It helps my ego." I rose. "Thanks for the bourbon, and the hospitality, and the psychology lecture. Thanks, too, for seeing through my Dennis Knowles ruse and listening to me, anyway. You're a nice kid, Fran."

"Thanks." She led me to the door. As I walked out, she said, "You forgot something, didn't you?"

"What's that?"

"Your glove. It's in the middle of my living room floor."

"I didn't forget it," I said, and I left.

We were playing the classic game called Murder.

Any number can play. You assemble your guests and you hand out a playing card to each person. The person who receives the Ace of Spades is the murderer. The lights are then turned out. Every player is free to move about anywhere in the darkened house. When the murderer sees his opportunity, he strikes. He taps his victim on the shoulder and hands him or her the Ace of Spades. The victim counts to ten slowly and then screams, giving the murderer a chance to get away from the scene of the crime. The lights are turned on, and the questioning begins. The questioning is handled by a person who was designated District Attorney before the lights were turned out and the murder committed.

The rules of the game are simple. The D.A. can ask any question he chooses. The object is, of course, to find the murderer. The murderer, having given his Ace of Spades to the victim, is the only player in the room without a playing card. When someone is accused, he must either show his card or admit he is the murderer, having no card. An essential element of the game is that every player must tell the exact truth when the D.A. questions him. Every player, that is, except one. The murderer. The murderer can lie to his heart's content. He can, for example, say, "I was in the kitchen leaning against the sink. I was nowhere near the living room where the murder was committed." He can be tripped up if everyone else tells the truth. Another player may have seen him in the living room shortly before the terrible deed was done. Usually, after a half-hour or so of questioning, the murderer has trapped himself in a web of lies. The truth, as being spoken by every other player in the game, is his undoing.

We were playing Murder.

There was only one difficulty.

Every player in the game seemed to be lying.

There was an added difficulty.

This wasn't a game.

I went back to the East Side and found a bar. I had no intention of getting drunk. I was going to pass a quiet afternoon until quitting time at the five and ten. Then I would go to Laraine's apartment and we would have dinner together and maybe we would make love afterwards and then eat a little more, the way the Romans used to do, and then make more love, and then I would ask her how come she'd been seeing Dom Archese, and how come she'd told me her acquaintance with him was a casual-meeting-in-the-street kind of thing?

I had one drink, and then another.

"How come, Laraine," I would say, "you lied to me?"

I had a third drink and a fourth.

How come you are picking up my gauntlet, Laraine, I would say, but at the same time you're telling me a flock of lies which can only make my job harder, huh? Or is this a part of the challenge? Screw up the battered shamus, spread confusion in the ranks, leave him doubting his long-unused investigatory powers, leave him sure of one thing and one alone, the woman in his arms, the one real thing in the world, more real than the ghost of Toni McAllister for sure, more real than a pack of liars and thieves and murderers, forget, forget, forget, I'll help you by confusing you, I'm a lying little bitch responding to the challenge of the International Society of Cuckold Pacifiers, come love me, Matt Cordell, come forget, come leave Johnny Bridges to rot in jail and twitch in the electric chair, nothing matters but the challenge, I'll make you whole again, I'll bedazzle the living be-Jesus out of you, come to my arms while I lie *with* you and *to* you, come.

I had a few more drinks.

The patrolman appeared at my elbow. I first saw him in the bar mirror, and I thought *Here we go. Vagrancy. Let's see your wallet, Mac, your identification, do you have a visible means of support?* No, you son-of-a-bitch, I have an invisible means of support.

"Matt Cordell?" he said.

"Yeah."

"We've been looking for you all day. Finally decided to come back, huh?"

"Yeah."

"Want to come along with me?"

"What the hell for?"

"The Skipper wants to talk to you." He paused. "It's about a murder."

Chapter Seven

We drove to the local precinct, and the patrolman waved at the desk sergeant and then led me upstairs to the Detective Division. The detective squad room was at the end of the hall—a bleak, colorless room with hanging light globes and desks and filing cabinets. "The Skipper" was a detective 1st/grade named Miskler, substituting for the lieutenant who was on vacation. We went through the squad room and then the patrolman showed me to a bench just outside Miskler's private office.

I cooled my heels on the bench for about ten minutes, occasionally looking at the frosted glass door that carried Miskler's name in peeling gilt letters. Finally, a guy in shirt sleeves and dangling shoulder holster opened the door, poked his head out, and said, "Cordell?"

"Yes. Detective Miskler?"

"The Skipper's inside," the guy said. "Come on in. Sorry to keep you waiting."

I went into the office. The guy with the shoulder holster had three counterparts inside, all of them in shirt sleeves. One of them was sitting behind a desk in the corner of the room. I figured him to be Miskler, the substitute boss. He was a big man with bright red hair and bright blue eyes.

"Cordell?" he said.

"Yes."

"I'm Detective Miskler. This is my squad, and these are some of my men, Jones, Di Palma, and Krutsky." The men nodded. I nodded back. "Have a chair."

I had a chair.

"What do you know about Johnny Bridges?" Miskler asked.

"Johnny Bridges," I said, as if trying to recall the name. "I don't think I know him."

"No?"

"No. Oh, wait a minute. Bridges, sure. I knew him when I was a kid."

Imperceptibly, the bulls were forming a circle around my chair. Miskler came from behind his desk and walked over to take the quarterback position, and the other bulls crowded in waiting for him to call the play. I wasn't on the team, but some of that old spirit was beginning to spread into my bones. I wondered if this were just going to be a verbal battering ram or whether we'd try for a run around end with rubber hoses. It was very hot in Miskler's office, and the crowd around me didn't help the heat very much. One of the bulls had a terrible case of body odor, but perhaps that was a planned part of Miskler's torture routine. I braced myself. If I was going to get hit, there wasn't much to be done about it. Bulls know how to hit, and they're usually big bastards, and there was no sense tangling with four of them. If we were going to play "What's My Line?" I wanted to be on my toes and ready for whatever questions came. I don't know if you've ever been questioned by four guys hurling questions in rapid-fire longhand. It can knock you on your ass, believe me, as sure as a punch can.

"When's the last time you saw Bridges?" Miskler asked.

"When I was a kid."

"How long ago was that?" Jones asked, or Krutsky, or Di Palma.

"About ten years."

"How old are you now, Cordell?" Di Palma asked, or Krutsky, or Jones.

"Thirty-three."

"Then you weren't such kids," Krutsky said, or Di Palma, or Jones.

"I guess not."

"And you haven't seen him since that time?"

"That's right."

"Where were you yesterday, Cordell?"

"All day yesterday?" I asked.

"Yes. All day yesterday."

"Drunk," I said.

"Where?"

"The Bowery."

"Where on the Bowery?"

"A park bench outside Cooper Union."

"Anyone with you?"

"No. I was alone."

"Until what time?"

"I don't remember. It was dark when I came out of it."

"Did you see Bridges yesterday?"

"No. I haven't seen him in ten years."

"Did you call the police yesterday?"

"Why should I call the police?"

"To ask about Johnny Bridges—using the name Joe Phillips."

"I don't know any Joe Phillips," I said. "Who's he?"

"He's supposed to be a lawyer. We think he's you, Cordell."

"What gives you that impression?"

"You went to see a private detective named Dennis Knowles this morning. You used the phony name Joe Phillips to get into his office."

"Did I?"

"You did."

"Who says?"

"Knowles says."

"He ought to know."

"He sure ought to," Miskler said.

"Is he the one who sicked you onto me?"

"In a manner of speaking. He thought he might be helping the investigation of a homicide. One hand washes the other, Cordell. He calls us often enough for routine help."

"I've got nothing to do with any homicide," I said.

"Don't you? Where's that paper, Fred?"

One of the bulls, Di Palma, Krutsky, or Jones,

handed Miskler a copy of one of the tabloids. Miskler opened it to the third page, folded it back and handed it to me. The story was headlined, "Harlem Tailor Slain."

"Read it," Miskler said.

I read it. "So?"

"That's the story we gave to all the metropolitan dailies," Miskler said. "You see anything in that story about the initials J.B. being found on the wall?"

I looked at the story again. I was beginning to get a queasy feeling in my stomach. "No," I said. "No mention of any initials."

"Then how'd you know about them?"

"Who says I did?"

"Knowles. He said you told him so in his office this morning. Now how about it, Cordell?"

"I guessed."

"Don't get smart, Cordell. How'd you know about those chalk marks?"

The quarterback had called the play, and the boys were ready to snap back the pigskin and go for broke. They crowded around me menacingly. This wasn't a vagrancy charge, and it wasn't practicing without a license. It was plain and simple accessory after the fact, and the fact was murder. I swallowed.

"Well, Cordell?"

"What happens when I tell the truth?"

"We decide whether or not it is the truth."

"Suppose I lose?"

"You're an accessory. You're an accessory anyway, so why not chance it?"

I sighed. "I was with Bridges when he found the body."

They were all brimming with questions now, Miskler, Jones, Di Palma, and Krutsky. They had me pinned and they wouldn't let me wiggle loose. In rapid-fire, each man taking his turn while the next man phrased his question, they let me have it.

"Why'd Bridges say he was alone when he found it?"

"We decided it would be better that way."

"How?"

"If I was left out of it."

"Why leave you out of it?"

"So that I could help find the real murderer."

"How do we know you didn't put the blocks to Archese yourself?"

"You know I didn't. I'm a goddamn drunk. I've got no motive for wanting Archese out of the way."

"Bridges has."

"Does he?" I said.

"Damn right, he does."

"What's the motive?"

"A little hanky-panky with Christine Archese, the dead man's wife."

"You've only got Dennis Knowles' word for that. I heard it differently."

"How'd you hear it, Cordell?"

"I heard it was Archese who hired Knowles to watch Christine. Not Bridges to watch Archese."

"Well, you heard wrong."

"Unless Knowles is in this, too, and trying to cover up."

"Knowles is too smart to get involved in homicide."

"So am I," I said.

"It doesn't look that way, Cordell. What were you doing with Bridges in the first place?"

I told him all about the cash register thefts. They listened blankly. When I finished talking, Miskler said, "It stinks."

"That's why you should know it's the truth. If I was inventing a story, I'd make it a doozie."

"And Bridges thought your help in finding the real murderer was worth lying to the cops, huh?"

"Yes."

"That's a laugh. You couldn't find your way into the I.R.T. with a token's head start."

"I'm a little better than that, Miskler," I told him. "I broke a few tough ones in the old days."

"These ain't the old days. These are the new days, and I read you for a drunken bum who maybe hired himself out for a quick bump job. How does that sit with you, Cordell?"

"It doesn't. It stands at the back of the theatre with its thumb up its ass."

"Watch your language," one of the other bulls warned.

"Then watch the stories," I said. "I'm not a hired gun. And I'll never be a hired gun, no matter how bad things get."

"You expect us to believe that crap about the cash register?"

"Believe it or not, it's the truth."

"Try this on for the truth, Cordell. Bridges is laying this Christine job, and she's quite a job, and I don't blame him. Archese knows, and they ask him for a divorce, but he won't play ball. They hire Knowles to tail Archese, but Bridges is getting impatient by this time. He likes the dame too much; he wants her as a steady diet. Answer? Get Archese out of the way. But who? Why not Matt Cordell, good old buddy Matt who used to live uptown and who proved he knew how to use the ass-end of a .45 when he beat up the guy who put the horns on him. Old Matt's down and out now, maybe he can use a C-note to keep him in liquid poison for a few days. Maybe old Matt would do me the honor of knocking off my partner for me."

"To quote you, Miskler, it stinks," I said.

"I ain't finished, Cordell. Bridges finds you and tells you the whole setup. You agree to do the job. You use the gun that was in the drawer outside, the gun Bridges owns. You come up to the shop and knock off Archese."

"I see," I said. "And Archese can't see too well, is that it?"

"He saw fine," Miskler said. "We checked his past medical record, just for kicks. 20/20 vision. What the hell are you driving at?"

"If he saw so fine when I was allegedly shooting him, how come he wrote Johnny's initials on the wall?"

"He didn't."

"No? Then who did?"

"You, maybe. It sure as hell wasn't Archese.

According to our autopsy report, death was instantaneous. He could no more write anything on that wall than he could breathe."

"Let me get this straight, Miskler. I was hired by Johnny Bridges to kill his partner, right?"

"Right."

"So I killed him, then picked up a piece of chalk and put Johnny's initials on the wall, right? Now why the hell would I do something as insane as that?"

"A smoke screen. It wouldn't be the first time, Cordell. The minute we ascertain that Archese couldn't have scribbled those initials, we're also ascertaining the killer *must* have scribbled them. And this automatically eliminates Johnny Bridges. What killer would be crazy enough to sign his job? That's the way we're supposed to think, isn't it?"

"Oh, Jesus, I don't know how the hell you're supposed to think. If this is a sample of what you come up with…"

"Give me a better story, Cordell."

"I gave it to you."

"And it stinks."

"And so does yours," I said.

"It's a shame I'm the cop, ain't it?"

"You going to book me?"

"You got a better idea, Cordell?"

"I've got a lot of better ideas."

"Let's hear them."

"Let me snoop around a little more. You gain nothing by locking me up."

"We gain a killer," Miskler said.

"Then Bridges is clear?"

"Not if he hired you, he ain't. It don't matter who pulled the trigger, you know that, Cordell."

"Okay. If you think I pulled the trigger, you've got me cold, right? Put a tail on me to make sure I don't leave town. You can pick me up whenever you need me."

"What do I gain?"

"You gain an experienced investigator who happens to have the confidence of most of the people who were closely involved with the deceased and the suspect. That should be worth something to you."

"The confidence, huh? Like the kind Knowles has?"

"Knowles is harboring a grudge. I once broke his nose. You didn't expect him to be good to me, did you?"

"It seemed *you* did."

"I made a mistake."

"I'm probably making one myself," Miskler said.

"What do you mean?"

"Take off, Cordell. You've got a tail, so don't leave the city. You make a move toward a bus, train, or an airplane, and you're on your ass in jail. Got me?"

"I've got you. Can I talk to Bridges?"

"What for?"

"To get his story."

"Why?"

"Maybe *he* put those initials on the wall."

"Sure. And maybe I did, Cordell."

I grinned. "You don't really believe I hired out as a gun?"

"I think out loud," Miskler said, "and I think a lot. You're still not out of this, so don't get cocky."

"You know what I think?" I said.

"No. What do you think?"

"I think the case has you stymied and you pulled me in because you need a real pro to crack it."

Mirthlessly, Miskler said, "Ha-ha. Take him down to see Bridges before he breaks into a soft shoe."

Johnny Bridges was being held without bail in a place known as The Tombs. It is not a very cheerful place, nor was Johnny in a particularly cheerful mood when they led him into the visitor's room. He sat down opposite me, the meshed wire separating us. He was already acquiring a prison pallor, which I am convinced is produced more by desolation than by lack of exposure to the sun.

"Have you had any luck?" he asked.

"Not yet."

"They wouldn't set bail for me," he said. "They really think I killed Dom, don't they?"

"The magistrate sets bail, and his failure to turn you loose in a free society is no reason to believe the case is being prejudged," I said. "Besides, the cops who are working on this aren't at all convinced you did it."

"How do you know?"

"I just had a talk with them. They're grabbing for straws. They even accused me of being a hired gun.

What it amounts to, Johnny, is that they're still trying.
They wouldn't have let me loose if they had any positive
leads. They're either hoping I'll turn up something, or
they're hoping I'll betray myself or another party. In
any case, this thing is far from solved." I paused. "Now
how about a little cooperation from you?"

"I've given you all the co…"

"Did you know that Dom Archese and his wife were
separated?"

"Yes," Johnny said unhesitatingly.

"Then why didn't you tell me?"

"I thought I did."

"You didn't. As a matter of fact, you said that Dom
knew you were going up to see Christine yesterday
afternoon. You told me, and correct me if I'm wrong,
that Dom had left a check for her and wasn't sure if she
knew where it was. He *sent* you there, you told me."

"That's right."

"Where *did* he leave the check, Johnny?"

"In the mailbox."

"Wouldn't she have found it without your telling
her where it was?"

"Maybe. Dom was fussy that way. He gave her a
check every week, like clockwork, even though they
were separated. He usually delivered it himself."

"When I asked you why Dom didn't phone her
about the check, you said you didn't know. You did
know, Johnny. They were separated, and he probably
didn't want to talk to her. Isn't that right?"

"I suppose so."

"Then you were trying to hide their separation from me."

Johnny hesitated. "All right, I was."

"Why?"

"Because it was none of your business."

"Even with a dead man laying on the floor? Even with your initials on the wall beside him? What's the scoop, Johnny? Have you been laying Christine?"

"No."

"That isn't the way I heard it."

"I don't care how you heard it. I'm telling you the truth."

"You're not in love with Christine Archese?"

"Of course not," Johnny said.

"Then why'd you go to Dennis Knowles?"

Johnny looked at me blankly. "Who the hell is Dennis Knowles?"

"The private eye you hired to follow Dom Archese. How about it, Johnny?"

He no longer looked blank; he looked positively flabbergasted. "Are you crazy or something?" he said. "I never heard of the guy. Why would I hire anyone to follow Dom?"

"Because you wanted him to divorce his wife," I said.

"Holy Jesus, where'd you get this…"

"Why else didn't you tell me about the separation, Johnny?" I shouted.

"Because it wasn't supposed to be common neighborhood gossip, goddamnit! And because I happen to have an interest."

"In Christine?"

"No! In Christine's sister. In Laraine Marsh."

I pulled up short. I thought about what he'd said for just a few seconds. Then I said, "What kind of an interest?"

"I've been seeing her."

"Object matrimony?"

"Maybe."

"In spite of the fact that Dom Archese was playing around with her?"

"That's a lie!" Johnny snapped.

The police guard at the door yelled, "Quiet it down there!"

I lowered my voice. "You don't believe Dom was seeing Laraine? You don't believe they might have been intimate?"

"No, I don't."

"How does Laraine feel about you?"

"I…I never asked her."

"What was your reaction to Knowles' report?"

"What report?" he said.

"About Dom and Laraine. Johnny, stop snowing me! If you want me to help…"

"I told you I don't know any Hennessy Knowles…"

"*Dennis* Knowles," I corrected.

"Dennis, all right, whatever his name is. I don't know him, I never met him, I never hired him, and I don't

know what report you're talking about. The reason I
didn't tell you about Dom and Christine was because I
might be in the family some day, who knows?"

"That didn't stop you from accusing Dom of being a
thief!"

"I didn't go to the cops, did I? I came to you."

"But first you went to Knowles!"

"Jesus, Matt," he said, "what's the matter with you?
I'm telling you the truth! I'm here because I'm suspected of murder! Do you think I'd lie to the one
person who might help me?" He seemed almost on
the verge of tears. I looked at his face. His eyes were
blinking, and there was a slight tic at the corner of his
mouth.

"Okay," I said. "I'll see what I can do. Don't get nervous. They won't be lighting a fire under you for a
while yet. Incidentally, they know I was with you when
we found Dom. So you needn't lie about that anymore.
They also know why I was there."

"You told them?"

"Yes."

"But you said…"

"I know. I had to tell them."

"You're handling it," he said. He smiled wanly. "Be
funny if I got the electric chair, wouldn't it?"

"Be hilarious," I said. "I'll be in touch with you.
Stop worrying."

"Sure," he said, and I left.

Miskler's tail picked me up downstairs. He was a tall
blond guy with shoulders like Primo Carnera. He

wasn't designed to be missed. Detective Miskler wanted me to know I was being followed. I didn't really mind too much. The wrestler behind me was undoubtedly carrying a gun, and his gun might come in handy some day. In the meantime, since I had no intention of leaving the city, I made no attempt to dodge the tail.

I went uptown to Laraine's apartment, the wrestler with me every inch of the way, keeping a respectable twenty-five feet or so behind me. I was going up the front steps when Laraine and Dave Ryan came out of the hallway. They were both bouncing along as if the world were made of pink cotton candy.

"What happened?" I said.

You could have cut Ryan's grin with a meat cleaver. "Tell the man, honey," he said to Laraine.

"We've got a big audition," she said.

"Tammy's Tavern," Ryan cut in, unable to contain himself. "In New Rochelle. Steady work every night of the week, and it's the jumpiest joint you ever saw! High-class, but solid. Man, there ain't a band in New York that wouldn't flip over this gig."

"You're going to New Rochelle now?" I said, disappointed.

"No, no," Ryan said. "The audition's being held at our rehearsal hall. Hey, man, what time is it anyway?"

I didn't own a watch, so I didn't lift my arm. Laraine read the time from her wrist. "Six-thirty," she said.

"The audition's at seven. Tammy himself is coming down. Oh, man, I'm as nervous as a cat." He crossed his fingers and then grinned again. "You want to come hear us, Cordell?"

I decided against it. "No. Will I see you later, Laraine?"

"I should be home by eight," she said.

"I'll be there."

"You're welcome at the audition if you want to come," Ryan said.

"No, thanks. I've got a stop to make."

"Well, come on, puss," Ryan said to Laraine. He took her arm and was hustling her off when she turned to me.

"Eight o'clock, Matt? You'll be there?"

"I will."

She smiled. "Good," she said, and Ryan almost yanked her off her feet, dragging her after him.

I sighed and headed for Christine Archese's apartment. In all truth, I still didn't know whose story to believe. I wanted to talk to Laraine but I couldn't very well ask her to miss an important audition. Besides, the talk could wait until eight o'clock. In the meantime, Christine might be able to fill me in on just what her relationship was with her husband and Johnny. Somebody was lying, that was for damn sure.

My tail stayed with me all the way. When I went into the building, he parked himself on the front stoop. I went up to the second floor and knocked on the door. I waited a few minutes and knocked again. There was no answer. "Christine!" I called. There was still no answer.

I yelled "Christine!" again, and then tried the door-knob. It turned easily. The door opened, and I stepped into the apartment. The apartment was very still.

"Christine," I whispered. No answer.

I walked into the living room. The door to the bed-room was ajar, and I went to it and pushed it all the way open. Christine Archese was wearing a sweater and slacks. The slacks were black and the sweater was white except for the red stains where three bullets had been plunked into her chest. Her eyes were open and staring at the ceiling. A pool of blood was seeping onto the floor in a steadily widening circle, spreading so that it almost touched the pillow which lay some two feet away from the body. I stooped and looked at the pillow. There were three holes in it, and the powder burns on the white pillow case told me that someone had wrapped the pillow around the muzzle of the gun as effectively as a silencer, muffling the explosions that had killed Christine.

I went downstairs. The wrestler was still on the front stoop, smoking a cigarette.

"Hi," I said.

He looked up, startled.

"You'd better come with me," I told him. "We've got another homicide."

Chapter Eight

I wasn't at all worried.

It isn't that I'm brave or anything, but this was one garland they could not hang around my neck. I had spent the entire day with various people. My alibis were solid to the core. Nonetheless, my wrestler called Detective Miskler, and I hung around until he arrived.

"You do this, Cordell?" he said.

"Not a chance. I'll give you a timetable even the Long Island Railroad can't beat."

"Let's hear it."

"Nine-thirty a.m., left an East Side apartment for…"

"Whose apartment?" Miskler asked.

This was no time for chivalry, not when a corpse was in the bedroom. "Laraine Marsh's."

"Spend the night there?"

"Yes."

"Go ahead."

"Ten a.m. arrived at office of Dennis Knowles, private investigator. Since Knowles later called you, you know damn well I was there."

"Skip the commentary," Miskler said. "Just give me the timetable."

"Right. Eleven a.m., left Knowles' office, went to Museum of Modern Art across the street. Purchased a cup of coffee and sat drinking it in the outdoor garden."

"Who saw you?"

"The guy who sold me the coffee."

"Go ahead."

"Eleven-fifteen a.m., called Fran West, investigator for Knowles, from a public phone booth in the museum."

"Did you go see Frannie?" Miskler asked, and his tone and his use of the diminutive with her name told me he was familiar with her.

"Yes."

"You know what she does for Knowles?"

"She's an investigator."

"Horse manure," Miskler said. "She poses in bed."

Chalk up another liar, I thought. Some girls are fresh and honest, I thought. Matt Cordell, appraiser of character. Fran West posed for pictures in divorce cases. She didn't pose for cheesecake mags, as she'd said. How do you do, Miss West? Welcome to the Liars Association of Eastern America.

"What time did you get there?" Miskler said.

"About eleven-thirty."

"What time did you leave?"

"About twelve-thirty."

"Where'd you go then?"

"To a bar uptown. I was there about a half-hour when your patrolman picked me up. Check with the bartender. The rest of my day I was with you, Johnny Bridges, and your tail. Am I clean?"

"You're spotless," Miskler said. "The tail's still with you. Get the hell out of here. We've got work to do."

I started to leave. Miskler's voice stopped me at the door. "I'm going to check with Fran West, and also with the bartender where we picked you up. You might keep that in mind."

"What for?" I said. "My innocence is as a child's."

"*Shnook,*" Miskler said, and I left the apartment with my tail wagging behind me. I waited for him in the street. When he came out of the building, I walked over to him.

"This is stupid," I said. "Why don't we walk together?"

He stuck out his hand. "Arthur de Ponce," he said, "detective 3rd/grade. I'm Puerto Rican. Any objections?"

I'm sure if I had any, he'd have knocked me on my ass in the gutter. Luckily, I didn't have any. "Matt Cordell," I said, taking his hand. "I'm Irish. Any objections?"

De Ponce grinned from ear to ear. With his blond hair and his bright blue eyes, he could have passed for an Episcopalian minister any day of the week. He chose instead to set me straight from go. His precaution was wasted on me, but I was certain many a loud-mouthed hater was taken slightly aback when De Ponce failed to fit into his stereotype of swarthy skin and long sideburns.

"Where to, Cordell?" he said.

"An audition in a rehearsal hall on 116th Street. You been on the force long?"

"Four years," he said.

"A detective so soon?"

"I'm a good cop," he said flatly, and I didn't doubt it for a minute. "Who's at the rehearsal?"

"A girl. Sister of Christine Archese."

"Where to from there?"

"Her apartment."

"You had dinner yet?"

"No," I said.

"Want to join me?"

"I'd hoped to eat with the lady."

"Mind if I pick up some sandwiches and Joe?"

I'd never met a civilian who used the military term "Joe" for coffee. "What branch of the service were you in?" I asked.

"Marines," he said. "I'll eat at the audition if it doesn't bother anybody."

"Who's going to argue with the New York City police?" I said.

We picked up the sandwiches and coffee and then went down to the basement room. The band was in full swing. A short fat guy in a brown Dupioni silk suit sat against one wall. He looked more like a pig than any human being I have ever met. He had a short pig's snout, and dull black pig's eyes, and thick little pig paws. A pinky ring sparkled on one of the paws. He wore an orange silk shirt under the brown silk suit, and the letters T.T. were monogrammed onto the left breast of the shirt where it showed beneath the open jacket. This, then, was Tammy Somebody. A nobody in a grey seersucker sat next to Tammy. As the band played, Tammy made an occasional comment to the seersucker suit. De Ponce and I sat at the rear of the room, and he commenced polishing off his sandwiches and coffee. Laraine sang a song, and then the band played a jump tune, and a cha cha cha, and then Laraine sang a torch song, and Tammy stood up in the middle of the song and said, "Okay, that's enough."

Ryan walked over to him, his trumpet in one hand. "How was it, Mr. Terrin?" he asked.

"Lousy," Tammy said.

"What!"

"I ought to charge you my carfare from New Rochelle. You got some nerve dragging me here to listen to a bunch of second-rate bums."

"Hey, watch it, Fat Boy," Laraine said into the mike, and then she stepped out from behind it and walked to him quickly. "If you don't like us, don't knock us."

"You cheap canary," Tammy said. "I've heard better voices in church on Sunday."

"You wouldn't know a voice from a hearse," Laraine said angrily, her eyes blazing.

"I know a lousy singer when I hear one," he said, "and I know a band from hunger."

"Go back to New Rochelle," Ryan said, joining the heated fray. "Get yourself an oom-pah-pah band that don't mind working for a..."

"I wouldn't allow this girl in my place," Tammy said, retreating toward the door. "A voice like hers…"

"Goodbye, Mr. Terrin," I said, rising.

He turned to look at me. Snidely, he said, "Who's this? Your arranger?" and he walked out, the seersucker suit following behind him.

"That bum," Laraine said.

"Goddamnit!" Ryan said. "Goddamnit to hell! Were we that lousy, Cordell?"

"You were damn good," I said.

"You know what this audition cost me? Jesus, I knocked my brains out getting stands for us, just so we'd look good. You know who stayed up all night painting those D.R.'s on the stands? And pasting on the stars? Me. Goddamn that son-of-a-bitch!"

"Forget it," I said. "You wouldn't want to work for him, anyway."

"The small guy never gets a break," Ryan said disgustedly.

"The small guy has to make his own breaks," Laraine said. "The hell with him. He'll sit up and take notice some day. I won't forget that bastard, that's for sure."

She turned to me. "Are you hungry, Matt?"

"Famished."

"So am I. Let's go."

I stopped to talk to De Ponce before we left the rehearsal hall. He was already wrapping his sandwiches, preparatory to following me again.

"Look," I said, "I expect to spend the night where

I'm going. You plan to sit outside until morning?"

"I don't know if I can trust you, Cordell."

"Do it however you want," I said. "Here's the address. I won't be leaving until morning. You can pick me up again then."

"What time?"

"Nine or so."

He considered it for a minute. "Miskler won't like it," he said. "I'll sit out front. It's summer, so I sure as hell won't freeze."

"You make me feel bad, De Ponce."

"I get paid for it," he said, and he grinned. "I'll call in for a car. Don't worry about me."

Laraine and I left the rehearsal hall. De Ponce was right behind us. He certainly would not freeze outside tonight. The heat that had been crowding the city all day long had managed to remain imprisoned in the brick and asphalt and concrete. There was not a breath of air to be had outside. It had been deceptively cool in the basement room, and now the jaws of Hell opened wide and a searing hot tongue of contained heat licked out and covered us instantly with sticky clinging sweat.

"Oh, my God," Laraine said. "Let's go back to the basement."

"And face a lot of long sad musicians?"

"I'm joking, but God! Was it this hot before?"

"It seems hotter after the basement."

"Let's hurry to my place. I want a very tall, cold drink. And I've got a fan we can put on."

We walked in silence for the length of the block. Then I said, "Are you very disappointed?"

"Not really," she said. "What's Tammy Terrin? Critic for the *Times* or something? He wouldn't know a band if it were around his throat and strangling him. As for singers, he's probably used to the drunks who wobble up to the piano and request 'Around the World' in the key of C minor. The Tammy Terrins of the world don't bother me."

"You sound bothered."

"If I do, it's only because I'm impatient. I want to get where I'm going—and fast."

We were on Second Avenue now. It was beginning to get dark, and the night noises of summer were descending around us. Night comes suddenly in the city, partly because the buildings obscure the sky, and partly because the lights seem to come on all at once, declaring an end to daytime. There is no watching the sky turn purple with dusk. There is no watching the sun sink below the horizon. It is day, and then it is night, and the night sounds start. The night sounds are the whisper of an enormous city. The radios tuned low, the muted hum of the television sets, the giggles of young girls standing in summer frocks on front stoops, the occasional beep of horns, the high moan of tug-boats on the river, and the lights which—soundless— seem to add to the medley.

We walked slowly because the city was truly hot and walking was an exercise that had not been designed for steaming pavements and sweating tenements. We didn't talk much because even that was an effort.

When we reached Laraine's building I said, "Don't forget your mail."

"I picked it up on the way home from work," she said, and she smiled.

We walked upstairs, and Laraine unlocked the door. We went into the apartment. The first thing I did was go to the window, look downstairs, and then pull down the shade. De Ponce had parked himself on the front stoop, apparently to wait for the car he'd ordered. I eased my conscience with the thought that he'd at least have the front seat of an automobile for the night. The first thing Laraine did was kiss me. Then, drawing away, she said, "Ahhh, that was good. The working girl's reward for a hard day's labor."

She was wearing a cotton suit. She took off the jacket to reveal a white blouse, opened at the throat. She wore a necklace with small simulated rubies, and she took that off quickly and dropped it on one of the end tables.

"Drinks?" she said.

"Yes. Where is it? I'll mix them."

"The kitchen," she said. "Setups are underneath the sink, ice in the refrigerator. My God, this place is suffocating." She went around the apartment opening windows while I went into the kitchen to mix the drinks. The open windows didn't help much. There wasn't a breeze in the entire city. But at least they created the illusion of being able to breathe. I brought the drinks into the living room. Laraine was sitting on the sofa, her legs propped up on the coffee table. I handed her the drink, a bourbon and soda with tons of ice. She took the glass and rolled it against her forehead and face, making small sighing sounds. Then she unbuttoned two buttons of the white blouse and pressed the cold glass to her bosom, rolling it there.

"Mmmmm, cold," she said.

I put my drink to more sensible use. I drank it.

"Been dating Johnny Bridges long?" I asked her.

She stared up at me. She had taken the drink away from her skin, but she had not buttoned her blouse. It hung precariously low over the swell of her breasts, a shaded valley between the raised mounds held tight by her bra.

"Who said I was dating him?"

"He did."

"You jealous?"

"No."

Laraine smiled. "Then why do you want to know?"

"For several reasons."

"Give me a few." She tasted the drink. "You made it strong," she said. "And don't give me the old rejoinder about strong drinks and weak women."

"I wouldn't," I told her. "Johnny says you were dating him. He seemed more than casually interested. I have also heard that Dom Archese was indulging in a bit of inter-family philandering. Any truth to that?"

"None whatever. Do you think I'm crazy?"

"I'm asking."

"Whether or not there was anything between Dom and me?"

"Yes."

"And I'm telling. No, there wasn't. Next question."

"The next question is back to the first question. Were you dating Johnny?"

"Yes." She rose suddenly. "Do you mind? I'm dying from the heat."

I didn't know what I was supposed to mind, and when I found out, I certainly didn't mind at all. Laraine unbuttoned her blouse quickly and expertly. She threw it over the chair and then went to sit by the window. The cotton skirt clung to her wide hips. The white bra held her breasts tightly. A high sheen of sweat was on the sloping flesh.

"Why'd you date him?"

"He's a nice boy. Why not?"

"Do you still date him?"

"No."

"When'd you stop?"

"Last month."

"Why?"

"I got bored."

"Was he in love with your sister?"

"Johnny? I doubt it. We never talked about her."

She rolled the drink against her breasts again. Then she got out of her chair and unzipped her skirt and folded it neatly over the chair, and sat down again wearing a half-slip and the bra. "I'm sorry," she said. "I can't take heat too well." She raised the slip over her knees and began rolling the cold glass against her thighs.

"Can you take shock?" I said.

"What kind of shock?"

"Your sister Christine is dead."

The rolling glass stopped. Laraine's face registered no pain, no grief. It simply stopped functioning. Impervious to heat now, impervious to cold, she sat in stony silence and stared at me.

"Yes," I said.

"How?"

"Shot."

"Who?"

I shrugged.

"I'm sorry," she said. "I liked her."

The room was silent. I gulped at my bourbon. Laraine sat motionless, still staring at me.

"Would you like another drink?" I said.

"No. I haven't finished this one."

"Want to talk about your sister?"

"No."

I stood opposite her. She sat. The room was very still. I could hear the ticking of a clock someplace in the apartment. It had probably been there all along, but I was hearing it for the first time.

"Great day, isn't it?" Laraine said. "Hot as hell, the audition blows up, and now you tell me this."

"Is that the order of disappointment?"

"Christine comes first," she said. "I was giving it to you chronologically."

"Were you close?"

"My father died when we were both kids. My mother died when Christine was twenty and I was eleven. We lived alone together until she got married. Yes, I suppose you could say we were close." She thought for a moment. "Am I supposed to call the police or something?"

"They'll get to you. I hope you were at the five and ten all day."

"I was." She paused and then seemed suddenly alarmed. "Except for my lunch hour. You don't think they'll…"

"Did you eat with anyone?"

"No. Alone."

"Where?"

"I came back here to make a sandwich."

"Do you usually do that?"

"Sometimes. It depends how I feel."

"Anyone see you?"

"I don't know. Matt, the police won't think I…I had anything to do with…with…"

"They might."

"But why? Why would I…want to…to…" And then the tears came. They came in a sudden rush, wrenched from the soul of Laraine Marsh. They started somewhere deep within her, and then rushed into her chest in a great heaving sob, and overflowed her eyes and caught in her throat until she choked with the overwhelming misery that suddenly claimed her.

I went to her. She did not rise from the chair. She

did not fling herself into my arms. Uncontrollably, she wept. Her hands clung to the moist glass in her lap. She did not touch her face. The tears spilled from her eyes, raining past her contorted cheeks. The muscles in her neck were tense. Her chest rose and fell with each new sob. The hands around the glass were white with strain.

I didn't touch her. I stood alongside her chair, and I said nothing, and I did nothing. Misery, despite the common adage, does not love company.

Slowly, the crest of her grief broke, ebbed, retreated. Her face was streaked with mascara. Her cheeks were shining wet. She sipped at her drink, choked on it, and began weeping again, softly this time. And then she drank again, and the tears stopped, and she sat in the chair with a silent stone within her, sweating profusely now, the constricting strap of her bra stained with perspiration.

She drained her glass and went into the kitchen. When she came back, the bottle was in her hand. She looked at me, and her eyes held mine, and she said in a cold level voice, "Do you believe there are some things a person must do, right or wrong?"

I shrugged.

"I don't care what you believe," she said. "There's something I've got to do right now. I've got to get stinking blind drunk. Can you understand that?"

She'd picked the right person to ask. "I can understand it," I said, "but the police might not when they get here."

"The hell with the police," she said. "I'm going to get so drunk I can't stand. You can stay if you want to see it. If you'd rather not, then leave."

"Someone's got to stay," I said.

"Why?"

"Who'll put you to bed?"

"I may get wild, Cordell. I may ruin you for life."

"I doubt it."

She poured three inches of straight bourbon over the ice in her glass. "Here's to murderers," she said, "the goddam world is full of them." She knocked off the three inches and refilled the glass.

"Not too fast," I said, "or you'll get sick."

"I want it fast and hard," she said. "I want it to knock me down." She drank the refill and poured again, gagging a little as the stuff went down. Then she kicked off her high-heeled pumps. Then she put down the bottle and pulled off the half-slip, and then she went to sit by the window in bra and panties, her feet propped up on the window sill.

She killed the third drink and then tossed her long blonde hair over her shoulder and shot me a backward glance and flashed the most evil smile since Eve grinned at Adam with the apple in her teeth.

"Come here, Cordell," she said.

"What for?"

"Come here and kiss me," she said. "Come kiss me," and she hissed the words, and I went to her and took the empty glass from her hand and kissed her.

"Mmmm, you," she said. And then she grinned at

me lopsidedly and said, "You need another shave."

I kissed her again.

It got cool later in the night. The breeze swept through the city suddenly, dancing through the open windows, touching the naked body of Laraine Marsh on the bed beside me. She didn't feel the sudden wind. She was out like a light, and there was a peacefully contented smile on her face.

Chapter Nine

We were eating breakfast the next morning when Detective Miskler arrived. Laraine had thrown a robe over her naked body. When the knock sounded on the door, she said, "Who is it?"

"Police," the voice answered, and Laraine whispered, "Oh, my God, I'm not even dressed."

"Go put something on," I said. "I'll let them in."

She went into the bedroom, and I went to open the front door. Detective Miskler looked bright and fresh, wearing a blue tropical suit and a snapbrim straw.

"Morning, Cordell," he said. "Sleep well?"

"Very."

"Little lady at home?"

"Getting dressed."

"I'm sure she won"t mind a few questions," Miskler said. He pulled a cigar from his inside jacket pocket and chewed off the end. "Okay to smoke?"

"I don't care if you burn," I said, and I grinned but Miskler did not grin back.

"Eight o'clock humor doesn't convulse me," he said, and he lit the cigar. "I've been up all night. Guess what the lab discovered?"

"What did the lab discover?" I said, playing the perfect straight man.

"That the gun which was used to kill Christine Archese is the same gun used on her husband. How about it, Cordell?"

"Interesting."

"Yes," Miskler said drily. "It is also interesting to note that the gun was a .38. From what the lab tells me, it was a Smith and Wesson."

"Yes?"

"Yes." Miskler blew smoke from his mouth. "Johnny Bridges told us he had a permit for a Smith and Wesson .38. We checked with Pistol Permits, and he wasn't lying. It seems, however, that the gun has vanished from where he kept it in a drawer at the tailor shop."

"I know." I paused. "You mentioned the gun the first time we met."

"I know you know," Miskler said.

"Well, Johnny sure as hell couldn't have killed Christine. He'd need more than a telescopic sight to hit her from The Tombs."

"I know."

"I know you know," I said. "Why tell me about the gun now?"

"Johnny's in jail," Miskler said. "You ain't."

"I gave you my timetable for yesterday, didn't I?"

"Only one thing wrong with it," Miskler said. "It doesn't check out."

"Which part of it?"

"The time you said you were with Fran West. I paid a call on the lady. She doesn't know you from a hole in the wall. Didn't see you yesterday, and never saw you in her life."

"She's lying," I said flatly.

"Maybe. Or maybe you are."

"You going to pull me in again?"

"I don't want to clutter up my precinct," Miskler said. "I'll let the Bowery cops get you on vagrancy."

"Thanks. All of which means you don't believe I have a damn thing to do with Christine's death."

Miskler shrugged, and then looked toward the closed bedroom door. "What's keeping her?" he wanted to know.

"She's taking her morning fix," I said. "You know how it is."

"Ha-ha," Miskler said mirthlessly. "Cordell, you are a very funny fellow. Is the Palace still booking comedy acts?"

"I think so," I said.

"Good. I can whistle pretty good. Think we can work up a double?"

Before I could think of a devastating rejoinder, Laraine came out of the bedroom. She was fully dressed, wearing a blue blouse and skirt, and blue flats. She had also found time to comb her hair and apply a coat of lipstick to her mouth. Miskler took off his hat and smiled. I half-expected him to bow.

"Good morning, Miss Marsh," he said, "I hope I'm not inconveniencing you."

"Not at all."

"I'm Detective Miskler, and my squad is in charge of the investigation into your sister's and your brother-in-law's deaths."

"How do you do?" Laraine said. She extended her hand, and Miskler took it. "Won't you sit down? We were just having breakfast. Would you like a cup of coffee?"

"Thank you," Miskler said. "I would."

Everybody was being so very tip-toey polite that I began to wish I wasn't in my undershirt. We sat down like a husband and wife about to discuss an insurance policy with a dear old friend of the family. Laraine poured a cup of coffee for Miskler.

"Sugar?" she asked.

"Thank you, one spoon."

"Cream?"

"No, thank you."

Miskler smiled. Laraine smiled back. I kept waiting for the Dorothy and Dick of the East Side to start their early morning breakfast show. In the meantime, I drank my orange juice and started on my coffee.

"Did you and your sister get along, Miss Marsh?" Miskler asked with the subtlety of Neanderthal clubbing a sabre-tooth tiger.

"Yes," Laraine answered flatly.

"Where were you between twelve noon and three o'clock yesterday, Miss Marsh?"

"Is that set for the time of death?" I asked.

"It's difficult to pinpoint it more accurately," Miskler said. "Yesterday was a very hot day. Heat and rigor mortis aren't compatible. How about it, Miss Marsh?"

"From twelve noon to one o'clock, I was here having lunch. From one until three, I was working."

"Where?"

"The five and ten on Third Avenue."

"What time did you quit work?"

"At five."

"And what did you do then?"

"I came here."

"And then what?"

"A little while later, David Ryan came to tell me we had a band audition. I went with him to the basement where we rehearse. Mr. Cordell can vouch for that."

"So can De Ponce," I said. "He was with me."

"Who can vouch for the fact that you were here between twelve and one, Miss Marsh?" Miskler asked.

"No one," she answered honestly.

"Then you could just as well have been at your sister's apartment putting a few bullets in her chest."

"I suppose I could have. But I wasn't."

"We have only your word for that."

"That's true. My sister and I were fairly close, Detective Miskler. The last time we argued was when we were both children. I thought motive was an important part of any murder investigation. Believe me, I had no possible reason for wanting my sister dead. I rather resent your implications."

"Yeah, well, that's a shame, Miss Marsh," Miskler

said, and it seemed as if he were going to say more, but instead he picked up his coffee cup and sipped at it. He was quiet for a few minutes. Then he said, "How well did you know Dom Archese?"

"As well as anyone knows her own brother-in-law."

"Better maybe?"

"What do you mean?"

"Did Mr. Cordell spend the night here with you?" Miskler asked, cocking his head in my direction.

"Yes, he did," Laraine answered.

"Then don't play this so damn naive. How well did you know Dom Archese."

"Not that well."

"Was there anything between you?"

"Nothing."

"Ever?"

"Never."

"Not even a kiss on the sly? A little holding hands? Nothing?"

"Nothing."

"Do you own a gun, Miss Marsh?"

"No."

"Did you know Johnny Bridges owned a gun?"

"How would I know that?"

"You were dating him, weren't you?"

"Yes, but he never mentioned whether or not he owned a gun. Why should I be interested in something like that?"

"What *were* you interested in? What did you and Johnny talk about on your dates?"

"Everything and anything. I'm sure I don't remember."

"Try."

"Everything," Laraine said, slightly annoyed. "How do you expect me to remember what we…"

"You're being unfair, Miskler," I said.

"Shut up, Cordell," he said. He sipped more coffee and turned to Laraine again. "What time did you leave the five and ten yesterday?"

"For lunch, do you mean?"

"Yes."

"At twelve sharp."

"And you came directly here?"

"Yes."

"What were you wearing?"

"What difference does it make what I was…?"

"Please try to remember."

"A suit and blouse," Laraine said. "Cotton. And tan pumps."

Miskler jotted it down. If his interest puzzled Laraine, it hadn't puzzled me. He was going to shop Christine's apartment building for a possible witness who'd seen a girl in a cotton suit yesterday afternoon.

"What color was the suit?" he asked.

"A sort of beige."

"What time did you arrive here on your lunch hour?"

"About five after twelve, I suppose."

"And what time did you leave?"

"About ten to one."

"Still wearing the beige cotton suit?"

"Of course."

"May I see that suit, please?" Miskler asked.

"I've seen it," I told him. "Not a drop of blood on it. Miskler, you're barking up the wrong…"

"May I please see that suit?" Miskler said to Laraine. She went into the other room and came back with the suit. "I'll have to take this with me," Miskler said.

"What for?"

"The lab would like to run some tests on it."

"Miskler, you're away out in left field," I said. "If you expect to find any traces of gunpowder on…"

"Oh, Cordell, do me a goddamn favor and shut up," Miskler said. He made out a receipt for the suit, gave it to Laraine, closed his pad, and then rose. "I'm going now, Miss Marsh, please don't try to leave the city, huh?"

"Why would I?" she asked.

"That's your business. I'm just telling you not to. Goodbye, Cordell." He went to the door, opened it, and then closed it behind him.

"What happens now?" Laraine asked.

"They'll go over your suit with a vacuum cleaner," I said. "If you fired a gun while you were wearing it, there may or may not be some traces of powder on the cloth."

"A vacuum cleaner?" she said.

"Yes. With a Söderman-Heuberger filter. You didn't fire a gun, did you?"

"No."

"Then relax. Even if you did, they don't always get powder. Cops like to make a big thing of lab tests. Sometimes they work fine, sometimes they don't."

"When do they work?"

"When there's something there to find. For example, if there's powder on your suit, the vacuum'll pick it up and when they place the filter under the microscope, they'll find it. As simple as that. *If* there are powder grains. Since there aren't, there's nothing to worry about."

"He was a snotty bastard, wasn't he?" Laraine said.

"You handled yourself beautifully."

"Thanks." She looked at her watch, "I've got to get to work. Will I see you tonight?"

"Yes."

"Where are you going now?" she asked me.

"As soon as I shave," I said, and I smiled, "there's someone I've got to see."

"Who?"

"Someone."

"Okay, keep secrets," Laraine said. She kissed me briefly and went to the door. "Tonight, lover."

The someone I had to see was Fran West.

I had not minded the young lady lying to me about her erstwhile profession, but I did mind her telling the cops I hadn't been to see her yesterday. I'm a firm believer in the theory that no one lies unless he or she is protecting some truth. Fran West had lied to the police, and I damn well wanted to know why.

Mr. Hitler was not sweeping his sidewalk this morning. Perhaps the pavements, as early as it was, were already too hot for him. I buzzed, was answered, opened the inner door, and trudged up to the third floor and apartment 3C. I pushed the ivory stud.

"Who's there?" Fran called.

"Cordell."

"Just a second." She came to the door and opened it. She was wearing Bermuda shorts and a white blouse. She'd apparently been awake for some time. She looked freshly combed and curried. "Come in," she said, "I was just having my second cup of coffee."

I stepped into the apartment. The air conditioner was still going on all six. It was like stepping into the freezing compartment of a Norge.

"Up early this morning, huh?" I said.

"A new leaf. Got up at eight and went down for the morning newspaper. I was just wondering how I could get in touch with you."

"Why?"

"You first," she said. "What brings you here?"

"I couldn't keep away from your hot little body," I told her.

"It's not so little," she said, the black eyebrows raising archly over the brown eyes. "Want some coffee?"

"Love some."

We went into the breakfast nook. This was turning out to be a ginger-peachy day with friendly breakfasts all over the sweltering city.

"Have you really got a lech, Cordell?" she asked.

"Oh, indeed, I have," I said as she poured the coffee into a giant mug.

"You came to the right place," she answered, smiling. "Honestly."

"Sure," I said. "Honestly."

Her eyes grew puzzled. "What's the matter, Cordell?"

"Several things," I said.

"I'm listening."

"One: you never did cheesecake. You posed in bed for Knowles."

"Okay," she said, shrugging.

"No argument, Fran?"

"Why bother? Is that why you're miffed?"

"Nope."

"Then spit it out."

"You lied to the cops yesterday. I told them I'd been here from eleven-thirty to twelve-thirty. You told them I wasn't. You could have got me in a lot of trouble, lousing up a legitimate alibi. Why?"

"Drink your coffee," she said, "and stop being so damn foolish."

"I want to know why you lied."

"I didn't," she said simply. "You're in swimming without your trunks, Cordell."

"You told Miskler I *was* here?"

"Of course I did. I backed you to the hilt."

"Why would Miskler lie?"

Fran shrugged. "Maybe he doesn't believe either of us. Maybe he thinks *you* knocked off Dom and

Christine. Maybe he thinks I'm mad about you and providing an alibi. How about it?"

"It's possible," I said. "Did he spend a lot of time with you?"

"About a half-hour, trying to punch holes in the alibi every minute."

"I'm still not convinced."

"Why would I lie?" Fran said.

"Why would anybody lie?" I said. "But everybody is."

"You can say that again. Here. I want to show you something." She spread the morning tabloid on the table and then opened it to page three. "Look."

"What is it?"

"This," she said.

I looked. Christine Archese's death was headlined at the top of the page. Her picture was beneath the story, and the caption was "New Victim." Beside that was a picture of Dom Archese captioned "Old Victim." And alongside that was a picture of Johnny Bridges, and it was captioned "Suspect?" They made a nice trio.

"So?" I said.

"Let's play Pick-The-Client."

"Go on. Pick him."

Her finger came down onto the page, landing smack in the middle of Dom Archese's forehead.

"Him," she said.

"This is the man who hired Dennis Knowles?"

"In person."

"*Not* Johnny Bridges?"

"Ah, but yes. He said he was Johnny Bridges. It

threw me when I saw the picture. After I read the story, I knew it was Dom Archese. Why do you suppose he gave Dennis the phony name?"

"That's not unusual," I said. "Lots of guys are ashamed to bring their dirty laundry to a private eye. If a man's wife is playing around, it's a reflection on the man—or so he thinks. So he'll go to an agency and say he's John Doe. In this case, Archese probably figured he'd kill two birds with one stone. Use a name that wasn't his—Johnny Bridges—and then pretend he wanted Dom Archese watched. The picture he gave Dennis was a picture of Johnny, wasn't it?"

"Yes."

"Sure. And he said it was Archese, right?"

"Yes."

"So he simply swapped identities. Which means he suspected Christine and Johnny of keeping house. That explains why he lost interest when you reported that the suspect was seeing a girl named Laraine Marsh. This told Archese that Johnny wasn't after his wife at all. He was probably ready to drop your services when he got killed."

"But who killed him?"

"I don't know," I admitted. "If Johnny and Christine weren't…"

The telephone rang. "Excuse me," Fran said, and she went to answer it. "Hello? Oh, hello, Dennis." She paused. "Yes, I saw it earlier this morning. I was just talking to Cordell about it. He's here, yes. Well, he just stopped by for a chat, is there any law against that? Oh,

Dennis, don't be a goddam fool." She paused again, listening. Then, very coldly, she said, "You're disgusting, Dennis. Goodbye," and she slammed down the receiver.

"Trouble?"

"Oh, he's a poop," she said.

"What's the matter?"

"He doesn't like the idea of my being up here alone with you. He thinks he's my father or something. He didn't seem to mind it so damn much when I was hopping into bed with strangers and getting my picture taken." She made a disgusted face and said, "I guess he just doesn't like you, Cordell. He put the cops onto you, didn't he?"

"Yes."

"I'd watch him if I were you. Dennis has a long memory, and his nose hurts everytime it rains."

"I'll be careful," I said.

"Seriously. He's a pretty vicious guy, and he loves you like arsenic."

"Okay, okay."

"So? Figure out who's doing the shooting yet?"

"No. Not Johnny because he was in jail when Christine got it. Not Laraine, because she was working. Not me, that's for sure. You don't think Dennis is involved in this thing, do you?"

"I wouldn't put it past him."

"Or this kid Ryan."

"Who's he?"

"Works for the tailor shop…or did until the time of the murders, anyway. He's really a musician, plays trumpet with a local…" I stopped, thinking. "Maybe I'd better look him up again."

"Have another cup of coffee first."

She poured the coffee, and since she was standing so close to me anyway, she kissed me.

"Nice?" she said.

"Very."

"More?"

"Not now."

"When?"

I shrugged.

"Okay, drink your coffee."

I drank my coffee and we chatted. Every now and then, Fran kissed me. It was pleasant. I didn't leave the apartment until about a half-hour later. I was thinking of the warm coffee and the pleasant kisses. I reached the second floor landing, and somebody hit me.

I've been hit before, and perhaps I've been hit harder, but in that instant this seemed to me like the hardest blow I'd ever received in my entire thirty-three years. I didn't need an anatomy chart to know that whatever hit me wasn't a part of the human body. Whatever hit me was hard and unyielding and was either metal or wood.

It hit me on the side of the head, catching my jaw-bone just below the right ear. I swung back from the blow, feeling hot pain spread into the entire right side of my face.

Staggering, I collided with the bannister, and then I

got hit again from the other side.

This was no fist, either. I saw what this was, and it was a blackjack, and it slammed down on my left shoulder, and then the fellow on my right swung his little surprise package again, but this time I stuck up my hand which turned out to be a mistake because the thing he was swinging was a lead pipe and it caught my forefinger and middle finger and I yelled but once in pain and then swung to the left where the blackjack was descending again.

I didn't know who was hitting me as yet. It didn't seem very important. My assailants were two sons-of-bitches whose only names were Blackjack and Leadpipe. I didn't need formal introductions to the people swinging the weapons. I threw a left jab into the face behind the blackjack, and then the pipe hit me in the ribs, and I went down onto the floor clutching for the bannister. I caught the wood and the blackjack came down on my fingers hard. I opened my hand, releasing the wood, dropping to my knees, knowing I couldn't allow myself to fall because the instant I was down they would pound out my brains with the pipe and the leather-covered six inches of destruction.

I tried to get up.

The pipe came down. I saw it coming from a mile away, and I tried to duck it, but I was kicked in the thigh at the same instant from the opposite side, and the pipe glanced off my shoulder bone leaving an angry throbbing dull pain and then the blackjack caught me across the bridge of my nose, and I went all the way down to the floor.

"Now give it to the bastard," a voice said, and I instinctively covered the back of my head with my hands, and the pipe crashed down against my wrists, and then the blackjack, and then the pipe, and then I heard a familiar voice shouting, "What's going on up there?" and I guess I should thank Detective 3rd/grade Arthur de Ponce for the fact that I'm still alive today.

Chapter Ten

They started down the stairwell. I caught a glimpse of them as they went past, both six-footers. The glimpse would be enough to last a lifetime. If there's one adage I believe in, it's the one about every dog having his day. Both these dogs weren't thinking of me at the moment. They were concentrating on De Ponce who was barreling up the steps with his service revolver clutched in his fist. Blackjack and Leadpipe went down the steps like a Panzer division. Leadpipe ducked his shoulder a little and sent it slamming into De Ponce's chest, knocking him against the wall, the arm with the revolver coming up over his head as Blackjack rushed past and clattered down the steps out of sight. Then De Ponce's revolver came down butt first onto Leadpipe's head, and he shoved him aside and away from him, ran to the first floor landing and yelled, "Halt!" at the same moment he fired down the stairwell. He fired again, and then a third time, and then wheeled as Leadpipe staggered to his feet.

The .38 came around level with Leadpipe's gut.

"Go ahead," De Ponce said, "make a break."

Leadpipe wasn't making any breaks. Leadpipe was

studying the .38 and working out fractions on the speed of a traveling bullet as compared to the speed of a hired mauler. Science won out. Reluctantly, Leadpipe raised his hands.

De Ponce walked over to him leisurely. He looked at him calmly for a few seconds, and then his left hand lashed out suddenly, catching Leadpipe on the face in an open-handed slap.

"You dirty son-of-a-bitch," De Ponce muttered, and then he viciously clamped one half of a pair of hand-cuffs onto Leadpipe's right hand, dragged him to the radiator on the landing, and fastened the other cuff to the metal pipe. Then he came over to me, kneeling.

"You okay, Cordell?"

I grunted.

De Ponce rolled me over gently, looked at my face, and winced. "Oh, Jesus," he said.

I nodded bleakly.

"I'd better get an ambulance."

I nodded again.

"Any idea who these bums are?"

"No. I...I think my right hand is broken."

"The other one got away," De Ponce said, almost to himself.

"I got a good look at him."

"So did I." He looked at my face again, unable to keep the pained expression out of his eyes. "I'll make my calls," he said. "Don't move, Cordell, huh?"

I didn't move. It was easy. I simply passed out.

*

There was a doctor with strong hands. The hands searched out every cut and bruise, cleaning, wiping, swabbing, patching.

There was a nurse with soft hands. The hands closed on mine gently when I screamed with pain.

There was the sting of alcohol, and the tight smell of bandages, the jab of a needle into my arm, and then the steady rolling waves of darkness, the pain ebbing, and then silence again, blackness.

It was dark in the room when I came around. An air-conditioner hummed at the window. There were clean sheets under me and on top of me. I blinked at the ceiling.

"Well," the soft voice said.

I turned my head on the pillow and sudden pain reminded me of what had happened. She sat by the bed in a crisply starched uniform. I knew that when she walked she rustled. She had bright red hair, the kind of hair you only find on an Irish girl. Her nose was dotted with freckles. She had blue eyes, and she probably burned a lobster red if she sat in the sun too long. A little white hat with a black stripe on it sat atop the close-cropped hair.

"How long have I been out?" I said.

She looked at her watch. "It's six o'clock. How do you feel?"

"Fine." I lifted my right hand to wipe the dry taste from my mouth. The hand was in a cast. "Is it broken?" I said.

"Yes."

"Badly?"

"Two fingers. They've been set. You'll be all right."

I nodded.

"Who beat you?" she said.

"I don't know."

"A Detective Miskler was here earlier. He wanted to talk to you. Doctor said he couldn't. He wanted to know when you'd be all right. He said he wants you to look at some mug shots."

I nodded again. I was beginning to realize how much plaster and bandage was on my face. I was beginning to realize that my right hand was broken, and what have you got left when you take away a man's right hand? You've got left. I was also beginning to feel a hundred little aches and bruises I had not felt before, all over my body.

"What's your name?" I said.

"Peggy."

"It figures."

"Why?"

"With that face, you're sure as hell no Brunhilde."

Peggy smiled. "I'll tell the doctor you're awake."

"All right."

She started for the door. "Don't try to sit up yet. You went into shock and…" She shrugged. "Well, just don't try to sit up. I'll get the doctor."

I didn't try to sit up. I lay looking at the ceiling, remembering the faces of Leadpipe and Blackjack and wondering who had paid for the beating. I felt miserable.

The door opened. Peggy entered the room, and a thin guy with a narrow face came in behind her. He grinned.

"Welcome back," he said.

"Thanks."

He extended his hand. I wasn't sure this was the doctor who'd treated me until I felt his grip. Strong and sure.

"How do you feel?"

"Weak."

"You're not the hero type, are you?"

"What do you mean?"

"You're not going to make a dash for your clothes and try to run out of here?"

"I hadn't thought of it."

"You're probably anxious to catch up with whoever did this job on you."

"I am."

"Let it wait until morning, will you? Or perhaps tomorrow evening. You've suffered some serious injuries. We'd like to take some X-rays now that you're with us again. There may be internal trouble."

"That's great," I said.

"Your hand is broken, did you know that?"

"Yes."

"Simple fracture of the forefinger, compound fracture of the middle finger. It should heal if the bones set properly."

"Let's hope they do."

"Yes. No hero stuff, Cordell?"

"Do you really expect me to make a reach for my pants?"

"The police tell me you sometimes act…let us say…impetuously."

I tried a feeble smile. Every seam of my face hurt when I did.

"Where *are* my clothes, doctor?" I said.

He gestured with his head. "The closet there."

I looked at the closed closet door. "I'd walk two feet and fall flat on my face," I told him.

"Just so long as you realize it, Cordell. You may be more badly hurt than you think." He smiled. "X-rays first thing in the morning."

"Right," I said.

"Are you hungry?"

"A little." I paused. "*And* thirsty."

"Miss Collins will get you some dinner. And a glass of milk."

"Milk?" I said. I tried to raise my eyebrows, but even that hurt.

"Milk," the doctor repeated. He went to the door and then out. Peggy Collins smiled. "I'll get you some food," she said, and she went out after the doctor.

I contemplated the ceiling for several moments. In truth, I had no burning desire to throw myself at Blackjack or Leadpipe. There wasn't much I'd be able to do about the beating, not now anyway. I've never been notorious for a wicked left, and my right hand was in a cast. It seemed important to me, however, that someone had taken the trouble to get me kicked around a little. That could indicate that I was getting warm. And the one thing that can cool off a beginning fire is lack of attention. You've got to feed it and fan it. The only thing I'd feed in the hospital was my fractured face. The only thing I'd fan was my feverish brow.

I got out of bed.

It wasn't easy. The aches and bruises all got up that old team spirit and tried to knock me back to the mattress again. I refused to budge. I held to the metal bedstead for a couple of minutes, waiting for my legs to tell me they could make it alone, waiting for the sudden dizziness to leave me. After a while, I decided to try the long walk to the closet. I tried it and fell flat on my face.

I got up again.

I held to the wall.

I waited.

Then I tried it again. It was better this time. I swayed across the room and then fell against the closet door, but I didn't drop to my knees. I waited another few minutes, gathering the strength to open the door and begin dressing. I wondered how long it would take Peggy Collins to dish up a hot supper. With milk.

I opened the closet door. I braced myself against the wall and took off the pajamas and then began dressing. I could hear the click-clatter of nurses' heels in the corridor outside. I wondered if Peggy Collins owned two of those heels. There was a sink with a mirror over it in one corner of the room. Fully dressed, I made my way to it and looked at my reflection.

I didn't look so good.

That is, possibly, an understatement.

They had covered most of my face with either plaster or bandage. They had not covered my right eye because it was not cut. It was however blue and purple and red, the lid swollen to three times its size. A nice hunk of plaster was pasted across the eyebrow, so I figured this was where the pipe or blackjack had landed. The swelling of the eye was only a secondary ailment, so to speak.

I kept studying my face, and then I made my decision.

I was going to crash Hollywood.

But first I had to crash out of the hospital. I went to the door. My legs were beginning to behave as if I had at least a down payment toward ownership on them. I opened the door a crack and looked into the corridor. Clean and white, it stretched to the elevator doors at the end of the building. A closed door in the middle of the hall carried the red sign exit above it. The door across the hall was numbered 407. Four flights down to the lobby. A nurse walked past. She did not see my swollen eye peering through the crack in the door. I listened for new footfalls. The nurse was standing at the elevator, pressing the button. The elevator arrived, the doors opened. She stepped in. I listened again for footfalls. None.

I opened the door and walked quickly to the exit sign in the middle of the hallway. I opened the second door, stepped onto the landing, and closed it rapidly

behind me. I leaned against it then because I felt dizzy
again. I waited. Then I started down the steps.

I didn't stop at the lobby. I went down to the basement garage, opened the door there and walked past
an ambulance and a man reading a copy of
Confidential, his chair tilted back against the fender of
the ambulance.

"Hello," I said.

He barely looked up. "Hi," he answered, and then
got back into bed with one of the movie stars. I walked
up the ramp and out into the street. It had cooled off a
little, but it was still pretty damned hot. The city
seemed quieter. Perhaps it was because one of my ears
had a wad of bandage over it.

I wondered where Dave Ryan was.

I decided to find out.

I bought a pair of sunglasses and a cheap straw hat.
Laraine Marsh had laid ten bucks on me the day
before and it was going fast. The money, she understood, was a loan. I wouldn't have taken it otherwise. I
believe in panhandling, but not from a woman you've
bedded with.

I looked up Dave Ryan's address on the slip of
paper where I'd jotted it when Johnny Bridges gave it
to me. I took a subway to 116th, and then a cab from
there to 120th. The cab ride cost me fifty cents,
including the tip. The Ryan apartment was on the
ground floor. A hardware-store sign on the door read
SUPERINTENDENT. I knocked.

The door opened instantly.

An Irish washerwoman type stood in the open doorway. She was not dressed like an Irish washerwoman. Only her face told me that. She was wearing her Sunday best. Her face was flabby, and her lips were badly painted, but she'd managed to preserve her body by adding poundage to it. The dress was too tight and the heels were too high.

"What the hell do you want?" she said.

"Dave Ryan."

"He ain't here."

"Who are you?"

"His mother. I'm on my way to Bingo. Are you one of his musician friends?"

"No."

"Well, he ain't here. What do you want?"

"Can you tell me where he is?"

"I don't know where he goes or what he does. That's his business. All I know is whenever he's here he's blowing that damn horn of his. I'm sorry I ever bought it for him."

"You have no idea where he might be?"

"None. I have to put on my earrings."

"May I come in?"

"What for?"

"You seem to be in a hurry, and I didn't want to hold you up. All I want to know is…"

"I don't know where Davey is," she said. "Why don't you look up his friend?"

"Which one would that be?"

She looked at me suspiciously. "Are you Irish?" she asked.

"Yes."

"Come in. We've got time for a drink before I leave."

I walked into the apartment. The kitchen was painted a bright yellow once. It was now painted with the stains of cooking. Mrs. Ryan took a bottle of whiskey from the shelf and poured two liberal hookers into water tumblers.

"Here's to the old man," she said. "May he turn over in his grave."

I raised my glass and drank.

"My husband," she explained. "The bastard died two years ago. Left me all alone in the world." She tossed off the drink and poured another. "I'm a passionate woman," she explained. "He shouldn't have died and left me on my own."

"This friend of Dave's," I prodded.

"Yes. Andy is his name. He plays a saxophone or something. The big curved thing with the black part you put in your mouth?"

"A saxophone," I agreed. "What's his last name?"

"Beats me," she said. "You want another drink?"

"All right."

She poured.

"I hate these damn Bingo games," she confided. "A bunch of old dames sitting around and hoping to make a killing. Big killing! Twenty-five bucks." She paused. "I'm a passionate woman, but I hate to go to bars and hang around. People think you're waiting to be picked up or something. Do you know what I mean?" She studied me for a minute. "I don't like to ask," she said, "but what the hell happened to you?"

"Somebody beat me up," I said.

"A strong young fellow like you?" she answered unbelievingly. "He must have used a lead pipe."

"He did."

"He did?" she said surprised. She made a clucking sound and poured herself another drink.

"Andy's last name," I reminded her. "Would you remember?"

"No. I'd remember if I heard it, but I never heard it. He's just Andy. The tenor man, Dave calls him. Listen, are you in a hurry to go anyplace?"

"I'd like to find Dave," I said.

"The hell with Dave." She grinned. "You've found his old lady."

"And a nice old lady, too," I said, grinning back.

"Let's kill the bottle and live dangerously," she said. The smile dropped from her mouth, and her eyes were suddenly pleading, full of loneliness, full of the empty life of a woman who'd once been pretty, the emptiness of Bingo games and pickups in bars and a yellow kitchen stained with cooking grime.

"Don't tempt me," I said. "I just got out of the hospital. A woman like you would kill me."

She chuckled. It was a dirty chuckle. She knew I was lying in my teeth, but she was enjoying it. "You're Irish, all right, you bastard," she said. "Have another drink."

"I've got to find this Andy character," I said.

"That won't be hard. When he ain't with Dave, he's in the candy store on the corner."

"I hope you win lots of money tonight," I said, standing.

"I've been going since the old man died," she said, "and I haven't won a cent yet." She shrugged. "Come back sometime."

"I will," I said. She knew I wouldn't.

I went out into the street, and I walked to the candy store on the corner. The guy behind the counter looked up when I came in, appraised the face for what it obviously was, and decided from go that I was a pushover.

"I'm looking for a kid named Andy," I said.

"Yeah?" He moved a toothpick to the opposite side of his mouth. In a booth at the back of the store, four young guys were sitting and listening to the juke.

"Yeah," I said. "Do you know him?"

"Andy who?"

"I don't know."

"I thought you was looking for him."

"I am."

"And you don't know his last name, huh?"

"That's right."

"This ain't the Lost and Found Department, Mac."

"The name is Matt," I said, "and cut the crap."

"Huh?" The toothpick was in the center of his mouth now.

"I said cut the crap! I'm asking a legitimate question,

and I don't need any wise-guy to talk right now." I put my right hand on the counter. "See that?" I said. "It's broken. But I've still got a left, and I'll knock you on your ass with it if you make one more wise crack."

"Tough guy, huh?" he said.

"Yeah. Tough guy."

"How'd a guy so tough get beat up so bad?"

"Six guys beat me up," I lied, "and all of them bigger than you and armed with ball bats. You want to take a whirl at it?"

He studied me for a minute. "Tough guy," was all he said.

"Do you know Andy?"

"I'm Andy," a voice from the booth said.

"The tenor man?"

"Yeah." He stepped out of the booth. He was a tall kid with a black crown of hair and long side-burns. He walked with the same hip, side-swinging walk that Dave Ryan used. "What do you want?" he said.

"I'm trying to locate Dave Ryan."

"Who are you?" he said.

"I'm a friend of Laraine Marsh's."

"Oh. Oh, yeah," he said slowly. "You been down to rehearsals, ain't you?"

"Yes," I said.

"Sure, I dig you now. Man, what happened to your face?"

"An accident."

"Wow!" he said, and then he made a sound like air

escaping from a punctured tire, and then he said "Wow!" again.

"Know where I can find Dave?"

"He said he was going on the earie tonight. Digging the various combos around, you know?"

"Which combos?"

"He didn't say."

"Downtown? Places like Birdland? Downbeat?"

"I doubt it. He was broke. Maybe he was heading for a session."

"Did he have his horn with him?"

"No. But he had his mouthpiece."

"A session where?"

"Hell, that could be anywhere. Lots of combos, you know, just to ease the drag of rehearsals, they get together in some cat's pad and just blow for kicks. You can really get the measure of a group when you hear them blowing for kicks. So Dave bounces around on the earie. He's half-interested in the competition, and he's half-interested in sitting in when the group is alive. You dig?"

"I dig. Where are the sessions?"

"Mostly West Side. Up on Lenox, around there."

"Where on Lenox?"

"Oh, man, I don't know. It's a homing instinct leads us to these guys."

"You busy now, Andy?"

"Just drifting."

"How'd you like to drift up to Lenox Avenue with me?"

He shrugged. I waited. Then he said, "I'd like to stop home for my mouthpiece first."

"Crazy," I said, and he blinked, and I could see he was mentally muttering over the imponderables that caused good legitimate musical language to sneak into the vernacular. Argh, what a world!

The pad on Lenox was jumping.

The musicians ranged from white to tan to brown to black. No one in that room was thinking about anything but music. I sometimes think all racial prejudice in the world would evaporate if everyone were taught to play an instrument and then allowed to join a gigantic international band. I've never yet met a musician, black or white, who has let color become any sort of a barrier. And this holds for musicians who come from neighborhoods where racial prejudice is taught from the cradle by well meaning parents preparing their kids for the hard knocks of life. It doesn't work on musicians. There's no room for hatred when three men or six men or a dozen men or two dozen men are blowing their separate sheets and making a conglomerate sound. The sound is the thing and music has its own color, blue or red or pale yellow or misty pink.

There was harmony in that room, and it didn't all come from the horns. The harmony was a thing you could feel in the jiggling feet and the clapping hands, the nodding heads, the wide grins when a man played a particularly good riff or rode a solo into the ground. I felt better the minute I walked in, and I was willing to bet that not one person in the room would ask me what had happened to my face. My face wasn't important. The music was.

The music was being made by seven men. Five of them were colored, and the remaining two were white. The other men and women in the room were either musicians or real music lovers. The piano player was obviously leading the combo, lacing intricate treble riffs into a steadily pounding bass, suddenly changing the tempo to a slow lazy blues, then leaping into a South American figure, setting the mood for the other musicians, changing the mood whenever he felt the boys wearying of the pace. One of the musicians clustered around the piano was Dave Ryan.

He blew sometimes in unison with another trumpet player, and sometimes in harmony. They switched back and forth from lead to second trumpet. The men seemed to play incessantly. When one grew just slightly tired, the melody was picked up by another instrument. If someone got really tired, one of the spectator-musicians would go to the piano, take his mouthpiece from his pocket, and pick up the discarded horn. It was a great big chain letter with the piano as its nucleus. I had the feeling they would keep blowing until eternity. I had the feeling that maybe this session had been going on in this apartment since the early days of New York, different musicians sidling in to take their places in a never-ending thing of sound. I had the feeling I was peeking in at perpetual motion.

"Oh, man, they're swingin'," Andy said. "I'm going to grab a horn as soon as somebody lets loose."

A long colored girl with magnificent breasts and splendid legs turned her attention to us. "They been at it since noontime," she said. "Jocko started fooling around with the ivory and then this guitar player dropped in, and man, the word was out. We've had every musician in New York up here today, I swear it. Jocko didn't even stop for supper. He's been pounding those keys all day." She paused. "I'm Clara," she said.

"I'm Andy."

"I'm Matt."

"I sing," Clara said. "No mike, though, and those cats are blowing too hard for my tiny voice."

I looked at her. She was sitting right then, but she must have been at least five-eight standing in her stocking feet. I found it hard to picture a tiny voice coming from her long, well-shaped body. She followed my eyes and then smiled, pleased by my open admiration. She didn't get insulted because I honestly wasn't trying to insult her. There are ways of looking at a woman, and there are other ways. And you can never fool a woman into thinking you're flattering her when you're really insulting her.

"You a musician?" she said to me.

I sat down on the floor beside her. "No," I said.

"That's a shame," she said. She paused. "What else is there?"

She was smiling. She had very brown skin and very

white, perfectly formed teeth. Her face was a narrow oval, with lidded almost-Oriental eyes and a flat broad nose. The eyes were brown. Her neck was beautiful. I'm not a guy who goes around appreciating necks, but this girl's neck was truly a work of art. I'm not trying to sound funny. Her chin was a good strong chin, and it flowed with the lines of a freeform sculpture into the delicate curve of her neck, swooping down to the full bosom in the sweater. She held her head erect, bobbing it slightly in time with the music. I doubted if she knew what a marvelous thing that graceful neck was, and I wasn't going to spoil her by telling her.

I looked over to where Ryan was blowing. His cheeks were puffed out, and he held that horn to his lips as if it were glued there. He didn't seem tired at all. I began to wonder if I'd ever get to talk to him. He looked as if he intended blasting away all night long. I closed my eyes and rested my head against the arm of the chair Clara was sitting in.

She asked me once, "You're not a junkie, are you?"

"No," I said.

"The glasses," she explained. "Lots of them wear them." She hesitated. "Not that it matters. Some of my best friends are junkies," and then she laughed at her own wit. I kept my head back against the upholstered arm of the chair, listening to the music. It was damn fine music. Clara began toying with my hair where it wasn't bandaged. She wasn't starting anything. She just felt like absently fooling with somebody's hair, and mine happened to be handy. She did it completely unselfconsciously, not even looking at me, simply listening to the music and absently winding a lock of hair around her finger, and then releasing it, and then winding it again.

It got to be midnight, and then it got to be two a.m. and then four a.m. and musicians and listeners kept drifting in and out, but Ryan would not release his grip on that horn. The apartment began getting light with the first early stabs of the sun, and still they kept playing. They were playing quiet stuff now, early morning stuff, stuff that came from deep inside a man's shoes, stuff that wept into a horn and told of busted love and better days and empty hotel rooms and neons blinking to a rainy night.

Along about six-thirty, Ryan put down the horn, yanked his mouthpiece from it, and walked over to where Andy and I were sitting. Clara was asleep in the armchair, her hand resting on my head.

"Oh, man, I'm bushed. My lip's gonna be like a balloon tomorrow. Anybody got eyes for some breakfast?"

"I could use some," I said.

"I'm gonna sit in as soon as somebody drops his grip on a tenor," Andy said.

"Come on, Cordell," Ryan said. "I know an all-night joint around the corner. This one is on me. Man, do I feel good!"

Gently, I took Clara's hand from my head and put it into her lap.

"Take her with you," Ryan said. "She's a sweet girl. She sings the end."

"She's asleep," I said. "Besides, I'd like to talk to you alone."

"Oh? Yeah?" He nodded. "Well, come on, let's make it. I could eat half a cow."

We went to a twenty-four-hour cafeteria two blocks down on Lenox. There were only four other people in the place. One was a junkie waiting for a meet with The Man, sitting and fidgeting at a table near the window. Ryan bought a mess of scrambled eggs and four onion rolls and coffee. I settled for coffee and a Danish. We pulled up chairs at one of the empty tables, and I allowed him the luxury of eating without being questioned. We were having our second cups of coffee when Ryan began expanding.

"I love music, Cordell," he said. "Everything else in the world can go, so long as you leave me music. I mean that. Dames, food, whiskey, everything. Just leave me my horn and a piano player like Jocko to bat out the chords. You ever play with a band?"

"No."

"Then you've got no idea. It's the only time I ever feel free, the only time I get that...that feeling that everybody's working together for the same thing. Oh, man, you can't beat it. It's people. It's people going, *doing!* And there's nothing can compare to it." He paused. "I'm sorry we didn't have a mike. This Clara Nichols is great. She's got this little voice that comes out like a whisper but she does things with it that curl your scalp."

"Is she better than Laraine?" I asked.

"Yeah. I think so, anyway. But Laraine's good. Make no mistakes. I wouldn't have taken her on if she wasn't. Well, I guess that's not exactly true. I suppose I would have taken her on in the hopes she was good. I mean, what the hell, that kid hasn't had a bed of roses."

"How do you mean?"

"Her and her sister—orphans, you know. That ain't easy. My old man is dead. It ain't easy. And with them, it was both parents. And they're girls. It's tough for a girl to get out there and make a buck."

"I imagine it is."

"Especially a kid as ambitious as Laraine. You think she digs this dime-store crap. Man, she hates it! She wants to sing! And she's good too, no mistakes." He paused reflectively. "Man, when I went up there the other day to tell her about that audition, I thought she'd flip. She'd only got home from work a little while ago, and she was sitting at the kitchen table with this tired look, drinking a cup of coffee. When I told her about Tammy Terrin, she ran into that bedroom and began changing quicker than I ever seen anybody move. And popping her head out of the bedroom all the while she dressed, and asking a hundred questions. Boy, was she excited! Well, you know. You met us in the street later."

"Yes," I said. "It's a shame it didn't work out."

Ryan shrugged. "That fat bastard. What the hell does he know about music? You think he'd appreciate Jocko if he heard him? Balls, he would! Laraine was pretty disappointed, wasn't she?"

"Yes."

"She shouldn't be. She'll get there. She's got a good voice, and she's also got drive." He paused. "You know her pretty good?"

"Pretty well."

"What I mean is…" He stopped. "Who cares? I was about to ask what everybody asks, but tell you the truth it don't matter." He shrugged.

"Good. Because I wouldn't tell you anyway."

Ryan grinned. "What was it you wanted to talk to me about, Cordell?"

"Your employment at the tailor shop," I said.

The smile dropped from his face. "Yeah. What about it?"

"You said you'd been working there about three months."

"That's right," Ryan said.

"That's a lie," I said.

He sipped at his coffee. "Who says?"

"Johnny Bridges says. You've worked there for six months, Ryan."

"Three months, six months. What the hell difference does it make?"

"This difference," I told him. "Somebody began stealing from the cash register six months ago."

"So?"

"So what do you say?"

"I say go jump in the lake. That's what I say."

"I say you're the boy. You probably made an impression of Johnny's key and then had your own key to the register made. Am I right?"

"You're crazy."

"Want me to tell you why you stole?"

"Go ahead. Tell me."

"You needed money for music and stands and possibly some special arrangements. You couldn't get that money pressing. So you got it stealing."

"Why should I steal from two guys I like?"

"Because you probably intended to pay it back one day. When the band hit."

Ryan was silent for a long time. Then he nodded and said, "Okay."

"You did it?"

"I did it. Johnny left his keys around one day. I pressed the register key in wax, and had my own made. Now what? A trip to the cops?"

"Don't be ridiculous," I said. "But there are a few more questions."

"Go ahead, let me hear them."

"Did you kill Dom Archese?"

It hit Dave Ryan right on his upper-lip muscle. He pulled his head back and opened his eyes wide as if the idea had never occurred to him, as if he thought it were completely ludicrous that I should even think of it.

"Me?" he said.

"Yes."

"Hell, no. Me? Why would I want to...?"

"Did you know I was onto you and the cash register thefts?"

"I thought you might have an inkling."

"Did you hire two men to beat me up yesterday?"

"No. Is that why your face looks like chopped meat?"

"Yes."

"I wanted to ask. But I figured if you wanted to tell, you'd tell."

"There could be another reason you didn't ask."

"Yeah, what's that?"

"You might have already known."

"Cordell, you've got me pegged all wrong. The only reason I dipped into the till was for my music. I love that music, man. You think if I had any loose cash around, I'd spend it on a beating? Man, I'd buy me a new horn!"

"These could have been friends of yours doing a favor."

"I don't have any friends who ain't musicians. And musicians don't go around beating up people. Do you want to know why?"

"Sure, tell me."

"Because anybody in the brass section can't afford a fat lip. And anybody who plays an instrument that needs fingering—and that's just about every non-brass instrument but the drums—can't afford to get his hands hurt. Musicians aren't famous for fighting. If you want to go around hitting people, you've got to expect getting hit back once in a while. And nobody who depends on his lip or his hands can afford that."

"It sounds reasonable."

"It's the truth," Ryan said. "I didn't have nothing to do with Dom's murder—or his wife's. And nothing to do with the beating you got, either." He paused. "What do I do about the money I stole?"

"You tell Johnny about it, and you return it to him with interest. That's what you do."

Dave Ryan nodded. "Yeah. Hell, I'm no crook. I'm a musician."

He said it as if he were very proud of the word.

I believed him.

Chapter Eleven

I left Ryan and caught a cab crosstown to the precinct house. It was now about eight in the morning, and I hoped I would catch Miskler either beginning a tour of duty or just ending one. A sign advised me to stop at the desk and state my business. I did so.

"My name is Matt Cordell," I told the desk Sergeant. "I want to see Detective Miskler."

He looked at me steadily, then plugged a wire into his switchboard.

"Frank?" he said. "Cordell's here." He paused. "Sure, right away." He pulled out his wire. "Upstairs, Cordell. You know the way."

I went upstairs. Miskler met me in the hall. He was chewing on a cigar, and a scowl was on his face.

"How's the walking corpse?" he said.

"Fine."

"Why'd you pull out of the hospital, you bastard?"

"I didn't want to cool off."

"You almost got cooled off yesterday," he said, "permanently. You looking for more?"

"I'm looking for a murderer. I didn't take a beating for nothing, Miskler. Somebody's scared."

"Or maybe somebody's sore. Stop jumping to

conclusions. I can think of a hundred reasons why I myself would pay to have you worked over."

"Maybe you did, Frank," I said.

"Don't call me Frank," he said. "Where the hell have you been all night?"

"At a jam session."

"We thought you might be with the Marsh dame. We woke her up at one in the morning."

"Why so late?"

"I wanted to see her in her pajamas," Miskler said mirthlessly.

"You know what I'm talking about. I left the hospital before seven."

"Sure. And would a smart buzzard like you head straight for the dame's place? We thought we'd give you a little time."

"Your concern is touching, Frank," I said.

"Don't call me Frank!" he shouted.

"What'd you get from Laraine's suit?" I asked. "Powder grains?"

"Not a trace."

"Then she's clean?"

"So far she checks out. She left the dime store when she said she did and returned when she said. But that still leaves a big hour in between."

"She's not your customer," I said. "She damn near died when I told her about her sister."

"Next time, leave us to do the telling, will you?"

"Sure, Frank. No offense," I said, smiling.

He didn't smile back at me, but neither did he tell

me to stop calling him Frank. "We're working on the boy who messed you up," he said. "Want to sit in?"

We started down the hall. On the way, Miskler said, "We've been researching our pal Archese. He wasn't exactly in the chips, but Christine would have been fixed for a year or two if she'd lived."

"His insurance, do you mean?"

"You know everything, goddamnit?"

"Bridges mentioned it."

"A ten grand G.I. policy. And, of course, there was his share of the tailor shop. The policy named…"

"Christine beneficiary?"

"Yeah. He also left a will leaving her everything he owned."

"How about her?"

"No will. Dames very rarely make out wills, haven't you noticed that? I guess they've got the American social setup pegged flat. The guy works his ass off keeping everybody in food. The dame works her ass off staying beautiful. The guy drops dead, and the dame goes on staying beautiful on the dough he left her. What dame needs a will? There isn't a man alive who'll outlive his wife."

"Cops are just cynics," I said, shaking my head.

"Up your bazoo," Miskler answered. "In here. Don't mind the rough stuff. We're not playing around with a decent citizen."

"I understand."

"You'd better understand, and you'd better keep your yap shut, or you'll be next."

"Just when we were getting along so nice."

Leadpipe was not getting along so nice. The cops were in their shirtsleeves, and they'd probably been giving him the business all night long. There wasn't a mark on him, but he'd taken a lot, and he was going to take a hell of a lot more.

"Who was your buddy, Paulson?" one of the cops asked.

"I don't know nothin'," Paulson said.

"Why are you protecting a cheap rat?" another asked.

"I ain't protecting nobody and I urgghhhh!" The grunt came when one of the cops hit him in the gut with a bunched fist.

"Open up, Paulson. You think that other bum'd take this for you?"

"What other urgghhh!" Another jab in the gut. Paulson's face went white. I kept remembering the lead pipe he'd wielded, and I wondered how many poor bastards he'd used that talented piece of metal on. I began wishing he'd never talk. I began wishing they'd beat his brains out. They kept pounding at him with questions and fists. One cop delivered a rabbit punch that I thought would knock Paulson's head off. He almost fell out of the chair on that one. Then he shook his head and sat up straight again, ready to take a beating for another hood who used a blackjack on people he didn't know.

The door opened. A uniformed cop walked in. "Call for you, Frank," he said. I followed Miskler into the squad room. He picked up the nearest uncradled phone and said, "Detective Miskler here."

He paused, listening. "Yeah, uh-huh, uh-huh, okay, don't touch anything, I'll be right over." He slammed down the phone. "You may want to come with me, Cordell."

"Where to?"

"Your floozy's apartment."

"What?"

"Laraine Marsh. Someone just tried to shoot her."

Laraine looked like a bird that had flown into a high-tension wire. Her hair was mussed, and she wore no lipstick, and her eyes were wide with fright. She wore a dressing gown, and when she let us in the gown parted over her knees to reveal a black slip beneath it. She threw herself into my arms instantly, and Miskler nodded sourly and said, "All right, what happened?"

Laraine began sobbing. I held her. Miskler looked around for a jug of whiskey, poured a jigger and handed it to her. Laraine drank it. I led her into the living room, and she sat on the sofa with her hands clenched tight in her lap, and again Miskler asked, "What happened?"

"Some…somebody tried to kill me."

"When?"

"I was…I was putting on my lipstick. At the…the dressing table. My bedroom. I've got to work today. I'm late now. Somebody…"

"Take it easy, Laraine," I said. "Tell us what happened as well as you can remember it."

"I was putting on my lipstick. I use a brush. A lipstick brush. I was...was bending close to the mirror when I...I..." She began sobbing again. Miskler and I waited. She was trembling as she tried to find her voice.

"Go on," Miskler said gently.

"I...I saw what...what he had in his hand. A gun. I didn't know what to do. I jumped off the chair, flat, on the floor, and he shot at me. He shot three times. He broke the mirror, that's hard luck, he broke the mirror, Matt, I'm terrified! Suppose he comes back?"

"Take it easy, baby," I said. "What happened after those three shots?"

"I screamed. I couldn't stop screaming! My neighbor down the hall came in."

"What happened to the man on the fire escape?"

"He dropped the gun and ran...down...away...I don't know, I didn't look out the window."

"Did your neighbor see him?"

"I don't think so. He was gone by that time."

"What did he look like?" I asked.

"A big man, very big. With black hair and...and a heavy beard."

"Did he say anything to you?"

"Nothing. He just...shot. And when I screamed, he ran."

"What was he wearing?"

"I don't know. A sports jacket, I think."

"Tie?"

"No," Laraine said. "I don't think so."

"White shirt?"

"Blue. A blue sports shirt."

"Think you'd remember him if you saw him again?"

"Forever," she said, and she shuddered.

"Let's take a look at the bedroom," Miskler said.

She led us into the other room. A dressing table was against the wall opposite the fire escape window. It was a small table covered with a chintz affair that hid the legs. A large mirror was on the wall behind it. Or rather, the remnants of a large mirror. All that remained of it, actually, was the frame and a few long silver shards. Three big holes were in the cardboard backing that had held the actual mirror in the frame. The mirror itself was shattered into a thousand pieces that lay on the tabletop and the floor. The chair in front of the dressing table had been overturned, and a box of face powder was spilled all over the floor.

"I...I guess I knocked it over when I jumped," Laraine said apologetically. "I'll get a broom and..."

"No, leave it alone," Miskler said. "Is that the fire escape?" He pointed.

"Yes."

He walked to the window, looked out, and said, "There's the gun, all right. A .38, Cordell." He spread a handkerchief over his fingers and gingerly lifted the gun from where it lay in a far corner of the fire escape, leaning far out the window to get it. Then he walked to me and held the gun out, the handkerchief under it.

"Smith and Wesson," I said.

"You bet. I'll tell you something else."

"What?"

"Before the lab even checks it, and before I call Pistol Permits for serial numbers, I can tell you this is Johnny Bridges' missing gun, and the gun that killed both Dom and Christine Archese."

"That sounds like a safe estimate," I said.

"I only make safe estimates," Miskler said. "Was this man wearing gloves, Miss Marsh?"

"Yes, yes, I think so. I thought it was strange, in this weather…"

"Nothing strange about that," Miskler said. "Only strange thing is that he left the gun behind. I guess your scream scared the hell out of him. If he was going to get caught, he didn't want the weapon in his hands. I meant to ask you. Did you ever see this man before?"

"Never."

"No idea who he might be?"

"None."

"Well, we'll let you look through some mug shots. Think it might be the baby who worked you over, Cordell?"

"Worked…?" and Laraine suddenly turned to me, as if seeing me for the first time and then said, "Matt! Oh my God, Matt, what have they done to you?" She put her hand up to touch my eye gently, and then she bit her lip, and I thought she was going to start crying all over again.

"He'll survive," Miskler said drily. "I'm going to

send a patrolman up here, Miss Marsh. Whoever fired those shots wasn't playing around. We may have scared him off, but maybe not. In any case, you need police protection."

"But I've got to get to work," she complained.

"He'll accompany you to the store and stay with you all day. I'm sorry. That's the way it's got to be. May I use your phone, please?"

"Certainly."

He went into the other room. Laraine came to me and kissed me and I held her close and again she shuddered, remembering the experience, reliving it, allowing it to frighten her all over again. Miskler came back into the room and said, "No necking, please. A patrolman's on the way over. Hang around until he gets here, will you, Cordell? I'm going to question Miss Marsh's neighbor."

He went out of the apartment, and I could hear him knocking on a door in the hallway.

"This man at the window," I said. "He wasn't the guy I tangled with Tuesday night, was he?"

"No. I don't think so."

"You're a lucky girl. He could have potted you."

She nodded. "Matt, I'm still shaking. God, isn't anyone safe? What's behind it all? Why Dom and…and Christine…and now me? What have we done? What has anyone got against us?"

I shook my head.

Laraine got up and went to the closet. "I want to finish dressing before the patrolman gets here," she said, and she took a black skirt from a hanger. "Stay, Matt."

I stayed. She took off the dressing gown and got into the skirt, smoothing it over her hips. It was a pleasure watching her. Then she went to the chest near the closet, opened a drawer, and took out a neatly folded black sweater that she pulled over her head quickly. She fastened a string of pearls at her neck and then brushed out her hair. She was wearing bedroom slippers, and she went to the closet, took them off, and pulled out a pair of black flats, which she hastily slipped onto her feet.

"I hate these ugly shoes," she said, "but I have to stand all day."

"They're not so ugly," I said.

She made a face and said, "Irrkkk" or something like that to express her loathing of the black working shoes. She lit a cigarette then, and we sat around chatting about small things, anything to keep her mind off what had happened, until the knock came on the door. The patrolman introduced himself and he and Laraine trotted off to the five and ten. Before she left, she made me promise I'd meet her there after work. I hung around in the hall waiting for Miskler. When he came out, I said, "What'd she say?"

"Heard three shots and then a scream. Figured it came from here. Waited a few seconds because she didn't want to get involved in any trouble, and then decided to come in anyway. Miss Marsh, she says, was sitting on the floor near the dressing table, with spilled face powder all around her. She was crying like a mad-woman. The neighbor suggested that she call the police. Any ideas who the bird might be, Cordell?"

"Nope."

"Your floozy have any?"

"No. And stop calling her a floozy, Frank."

"And stop calling me Frank," he said. "Why don't you go back to the squad and take a look at some mug shots? If we find your assailant, he may be one and the same."

"Maybe I'll do that," I said.

"I'll put in a call for some lab people," Miskler said. "See if they can dig up anything on that fire escape." Miskler paused. "Goddamnit, I hate mystery men, don't you?"

I nodded.

"Go up to the squad, Cordell. Start earning your keep, will you?"

"I didn't realize I was being paid."

"You could be in jail right now, you bastard. Thank your lucky stars I'm a kind considerate cop who always wanted to be a hobo."

I made a slight raspberry and stepped past Miskler.

As I went down the steps, he yelled, "Go on up to the squad and look at those mug shots!"

"Okay," I said. "I will."

I didn't.

Chapter Twelve

I didn't because I accidentally heard a radio as I passed an apartment on the second floor.

The radio was turned up rather loud. That's not unusual for a tenement. The radio was turned to a disc jockey, and the record on the turntable was "Lover."

It was like getting hit with the lead pipe all over again. It hit me in the gut, a solid club that caught my stomach and knocked the wind out of me. It was only a combination of notes, a trumpet with a muted sax background, not anything with real physical force, but it was "Lover," and I was weak all at once. I clutched for the bannister, and Toni McAllister Cordell was suddenly in that hallway with me.

There was a place. It was called Mike's but it could have been called anything because there are a thousand places exactly like it, and every pair of lovers has a place, and this place was ours, before we were married and for a while after we were married. It was a nice place, Mike's. We didn't know a soul there except the bartender and the piano player, and we never talked to anyone but them. We really didn't need anyone. There was always plenty to talk about, so we didn't search out conversationalists. The clientele of

Mike's was a mixed one. Television executives and playwrights and an occasional Broadway star sprinkled with guys who worked in the garment district and an old guy who lived on the block and who was a postman. It was a combination of a local bar and a haven from the local bar, and so the crowd was always mixed, but I'd never seen a fight in all the time we went there, except for the night I had one, and then of course we stopped going to Mike's, and anyway the end, the real end, wasn't too long after that—so I guess it was only fitting that Mike's should go down the drain along with everything else.

The place was on 31st Street, off Lexington Avenue. When we got married, we lived in a place on East 36th, which was convenient to the bar we'd come to think of as special. We'd been married two months when I had the fight.

It was a Monday night, I remember.

It was raining. It always rains on Mondays, anyway. Monday is the bitchinest day in the week and should be struck completely from the calendar. We were just sitting around the apartment, I remember. I'd just hired Parker, and he was out on a case, and I was looking over some reports from one of the other guys who worked in the office, and Toni was lounging around in a black velvet sort of thing with tapered slacks and a very low-cut top. She wasn't wearing a bra, what the hell the thing was designed for wearing around the house, and this was her own apartment, so the hell with you.

"Are you going to be busy long?" she asked.

"A few more minutes," I said. "Why?"

"It's such a dreary night. I thought we might go over to Mike's for a drink."

"All right," I said. "You go change. I'll be ready when you are."

"Do I have to?" she said. "I'll keep my raincoat on."

"Okay," I said. I was wearing a sports jacket and an open-throat sports shirt. I knew I wouldn't have to change because one of the nicest things about Mike's was its complete informality. Toni's costume, of course, was not intended for street wear but would do fine under a raincoat. I finished the reports, and then I helped Toni into her coat. It was one of these white jobs with a belt. She buttoned it across her throat, and it covered the skimpy top. All that showed were the tapered black slacks stemming from the bottom of the coat, and a pair of pony-skin boots Toni put on. I threw on a raincoat that looked nothing whatever like the raincoats private eyes are supposed to wear. Most private detectives dress like ordinary citizens. If you could spot an investigator by his raincoat, his value as an investigator would be absolutely nil.

We went downstairs.

It wasn't raining very hard. A soft misty drizzle covered the streets, hazing the lights, giving the city a muted look, the look of an impressionist painting. We decided to walk to Mike's. Toni took my arm, and we talked about rain a little and about the best kind of drinks to have when it was raining, and we decided to ask the waiter for a hot rum toddy. I bet Toni he wouldn't know what we were talking about, and she bet he'd serve it within five minutes. The stakes were a private matter.

Mike's was pretty crowded when we got there, but we found a table over near the piano. The bartender waved to us—a guy named Freddie—and we waved back. Emmett, the piano player, looked up and nodded and Toni and I both nodded back, and then the waiter came over to the table.

"Two hot rum toddies," I said.

"Yes, sir," the waiter answered, and he walked away.

"See?" Toni said. "I win."

"Just hold it a minute," I told her.

We waited. Five minutes passed. The man handling our table wandered back. "Sir, the bartender says he is not equipped to make hot rum toddies, sir. He suggests, if you care for rum, a planter's punch or a Cuba libre, or a zombie."

"I'll have rye and soda," I said. "Toni?"

"A whiskey sour," she said.

When the waiter was gone, I asked, "So who wins? He knew what we were talking about, but he didn't serve it."

"Nobody wins."

"And the stakes?"

She winked. "We'll work it out." She looked as if she were really anxious to work it out. I was rather anxious myself.

"The hell with the drinks," I said. "Let's go home."

"No. It's hot as the devil in here, isn't it?"

"I feel fine."

"You're not sitting in a raincoat." She unbuttoned the top button of the coat. "Am I showing?" she said.

"No."

"Dare I try another button?"

"Go ahead. Live."

She unbuttoned another button. "Okay?"

"Fine."

"I wouldn't mind, but I'm not wearing a bra," she said.

"Mmm, yes, I know."

"Stop it, you lecher."

The drinks came. Emmett finished his set and came over to the table carrying a glass of Scotch. "We've got a convention," he said. "A noisy bunch of bastards from Los Angeles."

"Where?" Toni said.

"Over there." Emmett pointed. "The funny men with the hats and the big buttons. Ha-ha, hilarious. I've been listening to them. They're telling toilet jokes. High-class humor."

"They don't sound too noisy," I ventured.

"They're resting," Emmett said sourly. "One of them requested 'Beer Barrel Polka.' He said, 'Hey, stop playing all this *cool* music, hah? Give us something hot like 'Beer Barrel Polka.' " Emmett pulled a sour face. "I'd like to give him a hot poker, all right, and you know just where."

Toni laughed in obvious delight. She had a laugh

that could be as dirty as they come sometimes, and sometimes as dainty as society-pinky-raised-for-teatime. This time it was dirty. I loved it.

"Give me a request," Emmett said. "Let me get the taste of the beer barrel out of my mouth."

Toni looked at me. She didn't just look at me; she invited me, she promised me, she claimed me. And then, still looking at me, she said to Emmett, "Play 'Lover.' "

"Great," Emmett said, and he left the table. Toni and I sipped at the drinks. I took her hand and kissed it, and Emmett fiddled around with an intro and then went into "Lover" with a vengeance. It was plain from the moment he began playing that he intended the song to last for four hours. He would play it in every style and tempo he could dream up. He would play variations and then variations on a variation. He would play "Lover" until it came out of the ears of the noisy men from Los Angeles.

For my part, he could have played it all night.

We listened, watching each other.

"I love you," I said.

"Shut up and listen to the music," Toni answered.

"Sure, but I love you."

"I love you, too, shut up," she said, without pausing for breath.

A guy who looked like a truck driver staggered past our table on the way to the men's room. He was wearing a blue suit, the tie yanked down, his collar open. He had thick hands covered with black hair. He almost knocked the drink out of my hand, backed off, said, "Excuse me, Bud," and then saw Toni. His eyes lingered on her a little longer than I thought necessary. He allowed a low whistle to escape his lips, and then he bowed to the table and went off to the john.

"Jackass," I said.

"He's drunk," Toni said.

Emmett was really warming up at the piano. "Lover" was taking on forms it had never known. We listened. Toni squeezed my hand every time Emmett fingered a particularly exciting riff. I was feeling great. And then the truck driver came out of the bathroom, and I saw that he was wearing the Los Angeles convention button on his lapel, and I saw his eyes seek Toni the moment he closed the door behind him, and I knew there was going to be trouble. I knew it the moment he came out of the john.

He walked to our table and stopped with his hands on his hips.

"You newlyweds or something?" he asked.

"Yes," I said, "we're newlyweds."

"That why you're holding hands?"

"Yes," I said. "That's why we're holding hands."

Toni had looked up at the man briefly and then turned away. She watched Emmett's hands as they reached for keys. The guy kept talking to me, but watching Toni.

"You're such red hot newlyweds," he said, "how come you're holding hands in a dumpy bar, 'steada being home…"

"That's enough, mister," I said, cutting him short.

"I thought newlyweds were supposed to be such hot numbers," he said, still watching Toni. Toni looked at him with a glance that must have given him frostbite of the toes, and then she turned back to the piano again, watching Emmett. The truck driver from Los Angeles didn't like Toni's glance. He'd probably never known a woman who could pack a slap into a look, and Toni's had not only slapped him but slugged him where he lived.

"Or is this a cold newlywed?" he said, looking at her with real contempt but failing even to scratch the icy armor.

"Mister," I told him, "you're stepping on my toes. Get the hell back to your table."

"Shut up," he said, without turning from Toni. I started to get up, and he added, "What's the raincoat for? You cold, missy? You got cold tits, missy?" He reached over for her just as I shoved my chair back. He yanked at the raincoat, snapping the buttons, pulling it open down the front, his hands tangling in the skimpy velvet top at the same time so that it tore open in a wide fleshy V that suddenly exposed Toni's breasts. Her face flared with startled anger. She pulled the raincoat shut in a swift furious motion, and that was when I punched the truck driver.

I punched him in the mouth. I have never hit a man more solidly. Not to the left or the right, but square in the center of his mouth. I felt his teeth buckle, and suddenly Emmett was playing "Lover" frantically and loud, trying to cover the fight.

The Los Angeles blade backed up against the piano and threw himself at me. I caught him with a left to the gut and then he unloosed his right in a roundhouse swing that clipped me on the side of the head and almost put me out of commission. This was no boxer, understand me. But he weighed all of 200 pounds and when that wild-swinging bunched fist collided with the side of my head I felt as if I'd been hit by the Lexington Avenue Express. I shook my head just as another roundhouse started, the left this time, catching me on the jaw and sending me reeling backwards.

I tripped then.

Staggering back from the second sledgehammer blow, I tripped over a chair and fell to the floor. I shook my head and then I saw the feet coming at me. The truck driver was running the way a football player will when he's kicking for the extra point. He stopped suddenly and his right foot went back and I knew that if he let it go at my head I was going to die of brain concussion. I tried to scramble to my knees, but the foot was back now ready for the kick, and I braced myself.

"You son-of-a-bitch!" a woman said, and then I realized the woman was Toni. She had leaped up from the table, forgetting all about the raincoat now, forgetting the torn velvet top under that coat. She picked up her heavy purse by the straps, and the raincoat swung open as she moved, and she came at the man, a bare-breasted fury swinging the bag at his head. His eyes popped wide at the frightening sight of her. He brought up his hands to block the swinging arc of the bag, and that was all the time I needed. Toni had broken his stride, and now I was going to break his head.

I was on my feet by the time he turned from her. I moved in close, ducking inside another roundhouse, working closer, closer, and then doubling him over, pounding at his soft underbelly with short hard jabs. And then I opened him up with a left uppercut and when he staggered away from that, I threw a straight right into his face and the man from Los Angeles hit the floor and didn't move.

There was a look of animal fury on Toni's face. Her lips were skinned back over her teeth, her eyes flashed with excitement. She was breathing harshly and raggedly, her naked breasts rising and falling. I looked at her, and she smiled curiously and then pulled the raincoat shut and, holding it closed with one hand, she said, "You should have killed him."

"Let's get out of here," I said.

Emmett was still playing "Lover" when we left.

I was out of the tenement hallway now.

It was brighter in the street, but not bright enough to kill the memory of that night, Toni leaping from that table like an aroused tigress, swinging her bag, giving me the time I needed. Not bright enough to kill the other memory, not two months later, the memory of her in Parker's arms, Jesus how had things gone so wrong, what had happened, how did two people so crazy in love go wrong?

I found a liquor store.

I bought a fifth and I found a hallway, and I began drinking. But instead of obliterating Toni's face and Toni's body, the whiskey brought her back bigger than ever, life-size, her smile and her laugh and her eyes and her hair and her sweetness and her anger and her wild passion. All of it came back, the night I'd found her with Parker, the brutal pistol-whipping, and then the crash and the wisecracks, and the guff from every son-of-a-bitch in town, the Mexican divorce, and the dull aching pain, the dull knife edge that ripped and ripped and would never stop ripping no matter how many women there were, no matter what, never, never.

I drank myself sick.

I let the anger build. I allowed it to start as a small black dot somewhere in my mind, and then I watched it spread, bubbling, spattering in larger black dots that merged until anger became the overwhelming reason for my being, until anger filled every corner of my mind with darkness, became an actual physical thing that jerked the fingers of my hands. I wished I could get at the truck driver again, but he was in Los Angeles. I wished I could get at Parker, but he was Christ only knew where. But Dennis Knowles was right here in good old New York City, and so the anger found a good solid focus on a real accessible hate object.

Like a drunken jerk, I left the hallway and went to the spider's office, and I didn't feel a bit like a fly until I threw open the door.

Chapter Thirteen

I'd shoved my way past the brunette receptionist, yelling at the top of my voice that I wanted to see Dennis. And then I opened the door to his private office, and Dennis looked up in real surprise, and I saw the other guy with him, and I suddenly felt very drunk and very incapable and very trapped.

The guy with Dennis Knowles was the guy who'd worked me over in Fran West's hallway with a blackjack.

"Well, well, well," I said, and the right hand in the cast felt clumsy and useless all at once, and I debated whirling and getting the hell out of that office, but something held me rooted to the floor.

"Haven't had enough, eh, Cordell?" Dennis said.

I shook my head sadly, the way a grandfather does when a favorite grandson has just used a hammer on his gold watch. "Dennis," I said thickly, "I really didn't think you would stoop that low."

Blackjack was standing alongside Dennis' desk, grinning broadly. His grin was an amazing thing. It managed to convey the purest innocence and the darkest evil in one lopsided twisting of the mouth. He still looked about nine feet tall. He was wearing an open-throat sports shirt, so the shoulders didn't belong to any padded jacket; they were his. The bulging biceps were his too. The blackjack sticking out of his back pocket didn't belong to his mother. He took it out and began slapping it on the palm of a hand the size of a tennis racket. I thought fleetingly of my own right hand. I began to sweat. The sweating had nothing whatever to do with the heat.

"I can stoop pretty low," Dennis said. "You shouldn't have come back to remind me, Matt. I'd almost forgotten about the nose until you showed up here and started asking questions."

"But you weren't man enough to try it yourself, huh?"

Dennis shrugged. "Why dirty my hands?"

I looked at Blackjack. "Your buddy Paulson is being worked over by the cops," I said. "It's not going to take them long to find out who you are."

"Yeah?" he said. "That's interesting because I'm leaving for Philadelphia tonight." He grinned again. "As soon as I take care of something I didn't finish proper."

"Right here in your office, Dennis?" I asked. "Isn't that a little dangerous?"

"Is it?" Dennis asked.

"It would seem to me…" I started, and just then Blackjack began advancing toward me. I wasn't afraid, but I was covered with cold sweat. Fear is a thing that can incapacitate even a man who has two good hands, and I had only one and couldn't afford to lose the power to control it. I waited. Blackjack, judging from his face, had nothing to worry about. He was coming toward a cripple, and he was going to pound that cripple into the rug. He was obviously a man who took extreme pride in his handicraft, and it irked him that De Ponce had interrupted him in the execution of his chosen profession.

I waited, and I thought of the Judo throws I knew, and I began automatically rejecting all those that required two hands. I was narrowing the list with amazing rapidity as Blackjack closed in. I hit on one then, but it didn't seem to me to be the best choice because all it would do would be to throw Blackjack and then I'd have to attack him after he was down and that still left me with my right hand in a cast. Unless...

I backed up toward the wall. Not too close to the wall, but close enough to accomplish two things. First, I wanted him to think I was ready to bolt so that he'd speed up and come rushing at me. Second, I wanted that wall close enough so that I could bounce him off it.

I accomplished the first thing immediately. Blackjack, thinking I was backing toward the door, began running toward me. I gave him time to build up enough speed and momentum, and then I took three fast steps toward him, throwing his timing off so that he reached me a fraction of a second before he thought he would. He could not stop, he could not pull up short; he was committed and he was ready to have his head collide solidly with a very thick immovable wall.

I dropped to my knees, ducked my head, and moved into the tunnel formed by his legs. He started to go over immediately. I grabbed the backs of his knees, shoved myself up simultaneously, crouching and then suddenly erect, his momentum helping me, and then I gave him the final shove which sent him headlong into the wall. I heard the solid *thwunk* when his skull hit. It wasn't over yet, though. Some guys have very hard heads. I flipped his body as I pulled free from his legs, so that he slid down the wall to a sitting position, and then I moved in on him and I kicked him hard, twice. I kicked him in the abdomen the first time and under the jaw the second time, and that was all. There was nothing further to do. Blackjack had just experienced a variation of the Rugby Capsize. I doubt if he'd enjoyed it.

Dennis Knowles was standing behind his desk with a shocked, awed, surprised, puzzled, and frightened look on his face. He knew this was just the warmup; he knew he was next. I turned to him and started moving toward the desk.

"Look, Matt…" he said.

"Look, hell, Dennis!"

"You broke my nose!" he said. "I had a right to…"

"Shut up, Dennis," I told him. "Shut up and thank God I've only got one good hand."

"Matt…Matt…can't we…?"

"I hope to hell you've got insurance, Dennis," I said, and then I stopped short because all the answers hit me at once. "Oh, Jesus," I said. "Oh, goddamnit to hell!"

Dennis blinked.

I blinked, too. Then I turned and left his office because I was going to face a murderer, and that's always the hardest part.

She threw her arms around me the minute I came into the apartment.

"Matt, Matt," she said, "I'm so glad you're here."

She was still wearing the black sweater and skirt she'd put on that morning. She had taken off the black shoes and her stockings. Barefooted, she stood on tiptoe to kiss me, her long blonde hair trailing over my hand.

"Just get back from the five and ten?" I asked.

"Yes. Miskler's cop was with me all day. I felt…"

"He's still outside," I said. "On the landing."

"I felt foolish," she said, "but I was glad he was there. I'm still frightened, Matt. Suppose that horrible man should come back?"

"He won't come back."

"How do you know? He may…"

"He *can't* come back, Laraine."

She looked at me steadily, and I could see the first dawning of suspicion in her eyes. "Why not?" she said.

"Because he doesn't exist."

"What?"

"There never was a man on your fire escape. Nobody took any shots at you. You did it yourself, Laraine. You knocked over your chair, and you spilled face powder on the floor, and then you went to the window and fired three shots at the mirror, threw the gun onto the fire escape, flung yourself on the floor near the dressing table, and then screamed like hell. There was no mystery man. You did it all yourself."

"Wh…why would I do a thing like that?" she said. Her eyes did not leave my face.

"For two reasons. One, you thought Miskler was a little too suspicious of you. You figured this would exonerate you completely. Two, you probably wanted to get rid of the one thing that would connect you to the death of Dom and Christine: the gun. So you tried to kill two birds with one stone. And you damn near succeeded."

"This is ridiculous," she said. "Matt, you're not saying…"

"I am saying," I said.

"Have a drink. You're…you're not thinking well. You're letting yourself…"

"I'm thinking fine."

She whirled on me angrily. "And you're accusing me of killing Dom and my own sister! How can you…"

"I know you did it, Laraine, and I know why you did it."

"Well, the police don't seem to think so. Miskler returned my suit today. He said they hadn't found any traces of gunpowder on it. He said…"

"The lab couldn't have found any powder traces, Laraine."

"No? Why not? They're supposed to be pretty damned effic…"

"Because you weren't wearing that suit when you killed your sister."

Laraine stopped talking suddenly. Anger left her eyes to be replaced by something else, a reaction to the threat I was now presenting. Imperceptibly, the eyes became a little more narrow, a little more cunning.

"What do you mean?" she said, but she didn't say it in outrage or in fear. She said it slowly and calmly, as if trying to ascertain exactly how much I knew before deciding her next move.

"I mean *this*. You told Miskler you'd worn the cotton suit and blouse to work on the day Christine was killed. That's a lie. Dave Ryan told me you went into the bedroom to *change your clothes* before the audition. Add to that what you told me this morning about wearing flats to work. You were wearing *heels* with that cotton suit, Laraine. I saw them. So whatever you wore to work that day, it wasn't the cotton suit. And you were smart enough to lie about it when Miskler brought it up."

She smiled. "I can't believe I'm listening to all this, Matt," she said gently. "I'm sure you don't believe it. Why in the world would I want to kill Dom?"

"Because he had ten thousand dollars' worth of G.I. insurance."

"But how would that help me? I'm not his benefic…"

"No, but Christine was. Look, Laraine, cut it out. You and Christine are orphans. She had no will. You're her closest living relative. This means her estate goes to you upon her death. And part of her estate is the ten grand in insurance Dom carried."

"But why? Why would I...?"

"You said it yourself, Laraine. You're going to make your own breaks, and all you need is talent and money. Okay, you've got the talent. And murder would give you the money. Ten thousand dollars. Enough to launch you. But I'm going to tell you something. You'd never have made it, Laraine. You'd never have got that network television show, or that Hollywood contract. Do you want to know why?"

"Tell me," she said.

"Because it takes a little more than talent and money. It takes brains. And a person who handles a murder obviously and stupidly is going to handle a career the same way!"

"Obviously and...!"

"All of it! For Christ's sake, I can't stand amateurs."

"Neither can I," she said angrily. "I don't see..."

"Do you think the police are absolute idiots? They handle homicides every day of the week, don't you know that? How far ahead of Miskler do you think I am? Ten hours? A half-hour? Ten *minutes?* He knows about the insurance, and he knows you're next in line. There's your motive, and once he's got that he'll add everything up and you're his target. Dating Johnny, for example. Why'd you do that? To find out whether or not Dom had insurance? To find out about that gun in the tailor shop drawer?"

She didn't answer.

"Stupid," I said, "from start to finish. Why'd you scrawl Johnny's initials on the wall?"

"Why'd you have to come into this?" she said.

"Answer me!"

"To throw suspicion on him!" she shouted. "Why do you think?"

"Sure. And what did you accomplish? You put a prime suspect in jail at the time Christine was killed. They knew he couldn't have done it, so who's their next likely suspect?"

"I don't have to listen to you," she said.

"Even killing Christine, for Christ's sake! A blonde like you, a girl who'd attract attention even in a neighborhood where she wasn't known, nonchalantly walks up to her sister's apartment in the middle of the summer when everybody's sitting outside on the front stoops, kills her, and then calmly walks down again! Jesus! How long do you think...?"

"I'm not that stupid, Matt!" she flared. "I went into a building on the next block, crossed the roofs, and came down that way. And I went back the same way. And besides, nobody heard the shots. I used a pillow."

"You were still stupid," I said. "Murder's always stupid."

"All right," she said.

"All right, Laraine."

"I want what I want."

"Sure. Everybody does. We just don't go around killing for it."

"You wouldn't understand, Matt."

"Wouldn't I?"

"I don't think you would." She paused. "What now?"

"Now I open the door and call to the patrolman who's on the landing. That's what now."

"No," she said. She took a step closer to me. "You won't do that, Matt. Not after what we've had. I know you won't."

"Won't I?"

"I love you, Matt," she said, "and you know it."

I didn't say anything.

She put her arms around my neck. Her eyes were misting. She parted her lips slightly, and her voice came in a dry whisper. "Matt, I love you. I love you, darling. Matt, please love me…"

"The trick you learned from the strippers in Union City," I said. "Try it on Miskler when he gets here. Maybe he'll think you're singing to him."

She shoved herself away from me viciously, and viciously she yelled, "All right! Call your goddamn patrolman! Get him in here and get it over with!" She held her head high, her eyes blazing. "I'm Laraine Marsh, and I don't have to crawl to a lousy drunken bum!"

"Your love just ran out, Laraine."

"Love? For you? In a free competition, I wouldn't have let you…"

"That's enough, Laraine."

"No, it isn't half-enough! The only reason you got closer than ten feet from me is because you were the only person to fear. I figured if I kept you busy…"

"No matter what you did, the cops would have…"

"Oh, shut up! Shut up, goddamnit! Shut up! Shut up!" There was naked hatred in her eyes. I had seen that kind of hatred only once before, in the eyes of Toni McAllister Cordell when I was hitting Parker with the .45. "Call your cop! Go on, you drunken louse! You'd turn in your own damn mother if she…"

"Maybe," I said. "But I wouldn't kill my own sister."

"You rotten son-of-a-bitch," Laraine whispered, and suddenly she began weeping.

I went to the door and opened it. I called down the hall for the patrolman, and then I gave him the story. It hurt. Don't think it didn't.

It was Saturday.

Tonight would be the loneliest night of the week.

It didn't matter much to me. I sat in the little park outside Cooper Union. I'd panhandled a dollar and a quarter that afternoon. There was a jug in my coat pocket, and a warm glow in the pit of my stomach.

Miskler had thanked me yesterday.

"Keep your nose out of murder from here on in,

you bastard," he'd said. I think there was a smile on his face. It was hard to tell with his face. He'd told me this right after they'd released Johnny Bridges, and just before they'd begun work on Laraine Marsh, the girl with the drive, the girl who was going to sing her way to the top by killing her way to the bottom. Well, maybe Satan ran a community sing. Or if she were lucky, she might get into the prison choir.

It was hot in the little park.

I sipped from the jug.

The traffic noises sounded muted and distant. That's the nice thing about the park outside Cooper. It's an isolated spot in the middle of a big bustling metropolis.

I drank from my jug. It was very hot, and I felt alone.

I felt very alone.

And Coming Soon From
HARD CASE CRIME!

Say It With Bullets
by RICHARD POWELL

Bill Wayne was supposed to be on a bus tour of the West—
but he was really on a mission to find out which of his old army
buddies shot him in the back and left him for dead.

Witness to Myself
by SEYMOUR SHUBIN

Tormented by memories of a day from his past, Alan Benning
returns to the scene of his crime—to try to figure out just what
he is guilty of.

Bust
by KEN BRUEN and JASON STARR

A businessman having an affair with his secretary discovers that
secrets can kill in this first-ever collaboration between the
award-winning authors of *The Guards* and *Twisted City*.

The Last Quarry
by MAX ALLAN COLLINS

In the first new Quarry novel in more than a decade, Collins
gives his hit man hero an assignment that may be the last one
he'll ever get.